STORIES TO TELL TO CHILDREN

I0729461

TWO LITTLE RIDDLES IN RHYME[8]

There's a garden that I ken,
Full of little gentlemen;
Little caps of blue they wear,
And green ribbons, very fair.
          (Flax.)

From house to house he goes,
A messenger small and slight,
And whether it rains or snows,
He sleeps outside in the night.
          (The path.)

THE LITTLE YELLOW TULIP

Once there was a little yellow Tulip, and she lived down in a little dark house under the ground. One day she was sitting there, all by herself, and it was very still. Suddenly, she heard a little *tap,tap,tap* , at the door.

"Who is that?" she said.

"It's the Rain, and I want to come in," said a soft, sad, little voice.

"No, you can't come in," the little Tulip said.

By and by she heard another little *tap,tap,tap* on the window-pane.

"Who is there?" she said.

The same soft little voice answered, "It's the Rain, and I want to come in!"

"No, you can't come in," said the little Tulip.

Then it was very still for a long time. At last, there came a little rustling, whispering sound, all round the window: *rustle,whisper ,whisper* .

"Who is there?" said the little Tulip.

"It's the Sunshine," said a little, soft, cheery voice, "and I want to come in!"

"N—no," said the little Tulip, "you can't come in." And she sat still again.

Pretty soon she heard the sweet little rustling noise at the keyhole.

"Who is there?" she said.

"It's the Sunshine," said the cheery little voice, "and I want to come in, I want to come in!"

"No, no," said the little Tulip, "you cannot come in."

By and by, as she sat so still, she heard *tap, tap, tap,* and *rustle, whisper, rustle,* up and down the window-pane, and on the door and at the keyhole.

"Whoisther e?" she said.

"It's the Rain and the Sun, the Rain and the Sun," said two little voices, together, "and we want to come in! We want to come in! We want to come in!"

"Dear, dear!" said the little Tulip, "if there are two of you, I s'pose I shall have to let you in."

So she opened the door a little wee crack, and in they came. And one took one of her little hands, and the other took her other little hand, and they ran, ran, ran with her right up to the top of the ground. Then they said,—

"Poke your head through!"

So she poked her head through; and she was in the midst of a beautiful garden. It was early springtime, and few other flowers were to be seen; but she had the birds to sing to her and the sun to shine upon her pretty yellow head. She was so pleased, too, when the children exclaimed with pleasure that now they knew that the beautiful spring had come!

THE COCK-A-DOO-DLE-DOO[9]

A very little boy made this story up "out of his head," and told it to his papa. I think you littlest ones will like it; I do.

Once upon a time there was a little boy, and he wanted to be a cock-a-doo-dle-doo. So he was a cock-a-doo-dle-doo. And he wanted to fly up into the sky. So he did fly up into the sky. And he wanted to get wings and a tail So he did get some wings and a tail.

THE CLOUD[10]

One hot summer morning a little Cloud rose out of the sea and floated lightly and happily across the blue sky. Far below lay the earth, brown, dry, and desolate, from drought. The little Cloud could see the poor people of the earth working and suffering in the hot fields, while she herself floated on the morning breeze, hither and thither, without a care.

"Oh, if I could only help the poor people down there!" she thought. "If I could but make their work easier, or give the hungry ones food, or the thirsty a drink!"

And as the day passed, and the Cloud became larger, this wish to do something for the people of earth was ever greater in her heart.

On earth it grew hotter and hotter; the sun burned down so fiercely that the people were fainting in its rays; it seemed as if they must die of heat, and yet they were obliged to go on with their work, for they were very poor. Sometimes they stood and looked up at the Cloud, as if they were praying, and saying, "Ah, if you could help us!"

"I will help you; I will!" said the Cloud. And she began to sink softly down toward the earth.

But suddenly, as she floated down, she remembered something which had been told her when she was a tiny Cloud-child, in the lap of Mother Ocean: it had been whispered that if the Clouds go too near the earth they die. When she remembered this she held herself from sinking, and swayed here and there on the breeze, thinking,—thinking. But at last she stood quite still, and spoke boldly and proudly. She said, "Men of earth, I will help you, come what may!"

The thought made her suddenly marvellously big and strong and powerful. Never had she dreamed that she could be so big. Like a mighty angel of blessing she stood above the earth, and lifted her head and spread her wings far over the fields and woods. She was so great, so majestic, that men and animals were awe-struck at the sight; the trees and the grasses bowed before her; yet all the earth-creatures felt that she meant them well.

"Yes, I will help you," cried the Cloud once more. "Take me to yourselves; I will give my life for you!"

As she said the words a wonderful light glowed from her heart, the sound of thunder rolled through the sky, and a love greater than words can tell filled the Cloud; down, down, close to the earth she swept, and gave up her life in a blessed, healing shower of rain.

That rain was the Cloud's great deed; it was her death, too; but it was also her glory. Over the whole country-side, as far as the rain fell, a lovely rainbow sprang its arch, and all the brightest rays of heaven made its colours; it was the last greeting of a love so great that it sacrificed itself.

Soon that, too, was gone, but long, long afterward the men and animals who were saved by the Cloud kept her blessing in their hearts.

THE LITTLE RED HEN

The little Red Hen was in the farmyard with her chickens, when she found a grain of wheat.

"Who will plant this wheat?" she said.

"Not I," said the Goose.

"Not I," said the Duck.

"I will, then," said the little Red Hen, and she planted the grain of wheat.

When the wheat was ripe she said, "Who will take this wheat to the mill?"

"Not I," said the Goose.

"Not I," said the Duck.

"I will, then," said the little Red Hen, and she took the wheat to the mill.

When she brought the flour home she said, "Who will make some bread with this flour?"

"Not I," said the Goose.

"Not I," said the Duck.

"I will, then," said the little Red Hen.

When the bread was baked, she said, "Who will eat this bread?"

"I will," said the Goose.

"I will," said the Duck.

"No, you won't," said the little Red Hen. "I shall eat it myself. Cluck! cluck!" And she called her chickens to help her.

THE GINGERBREAD MAN[11]

Once upon a time there was a little old woman and a little old man, and they lived all alone in a little old house. They hadn't any little girls or any little boys, at all. So one day, the little old woman made a boy out of gingerbread; she made him a chocolate jacket, and put raisins on it for buttons; his eyes were made of fine, fat currants; his mouth was made of rose-coloured sugar; and he had a gay little cap of orange sugar-candy. When the little old woman had rolled him out, and dressed him up, and pinched his gingerbread shoes into shape, she put him in a pan; then she put the pan in the oven and shut the door; and she thought, "Now I shall have a little boy of my own."

When it was time for the Gingerbread Boy to be done she opened the oven door and pulled out the pan. Out jumped the little Gingerbread Boy on to the floor, and away he ran, out of the door and down the street! The little old woman and the little old man ran after him as fast as they could, but he just laughed, and shouted,—

"Run! run! as fast as you can!

"You can't catch me, I'm the Gingerbread Man!"

And they couldn't catch him.

The little Gingerbread Boy ran on and on, until he came to a cow, by the roadside. "Stop, little Gingerbread Boy," said the cow; "I want to eat you." The little Gingerbread Boy laughed and said,—

"I have run away from a little old woman,

"And a little old man,

"And I can run away from you, I can!"

And, as the cow chased him, he looked over his shoulder and cried,—

"Run! run! as fast as you can!

"You can't catch me, I'm the Gingerbread Man!"

And the cow couldn't catch him.

The little Gingerbread Boy ran on, and on, and on, till he came to a horse, in the pasture. "Please stop, little Gingerbread Boy," said the horse, "you look very good to eat." But the little Gingerbread Boy laughed out loud. "Oho! oho!" he said,—

"I have run away from a little old woman,

"A little old man,

"A cow,

"And I can run away from you, I can!"

And, as the horse chased him, he looked over his shoulder and cried,—

"Run! run! as fast as you can!

"You can't catch me, I'm the Gingerbread Man!"

And the horse couldn't catch him.

By and by the little Gingerbread Boy came to a barn full of threshers. When the threshers smelt the Gingerbread Boy, they tried to pick him up, and said, "Don't run so fast, little Gingerbread Boy; you look very good to eat."

But the little Gingerbread Boy ran harder than ever, and as he ran he cried out,—

"I have run away from a little old woman,

"A little old man,

"A cow,

"A horse,

"And I can run away from you, I can!"

And when he found that he was ahead of the threshers, he turned and shouted back to them,—

"Run! run! as fast as you can!

"You can't catch me, I'm the Gingerbread Man!"

And the threshers couldn't catch him.

Then the little Gingerbread Boy ran faster than ever. He ran and ran until he came to a field full of mowers. When the mowers saw how fine he looked, they ran after him, calling out, "Wait a bit! wait a bit, little Gingerbread Boy, we wish to eat you!" But the little Gingerbread Boy laughed harder than ever, and ran like the wind. "Oho! oho!" he said,—

"I have run away from a little old woman,

"A little old man,

"A cow,

"A horse,

"A barn full of threshers,

"And I can run away from you, I can!"

And when he found that he was ahead of the mowers, he turned and shouted back to them,—

"Run! run! as fast as you can!

"You can't catch me, I'm the Gingerbread Man!"

And the mowers couldn't catch him.

By this time the little Gingerbread Boy was so proud that he didn't think anybody could catch him. Pretty soon he saw a fox coming across a field. The fox looked at him and began to run. But the little Gingerbread Boy shouted across to him, "You can't catch me!" The fox began to run faster, and the little Gingerbread Boy ran faster, and as he ran he chuckled,—

"I have run away from a little old woman,

"A little old man,

"A cow,

"A horse,

"A barn full of threshers,

"A field full of mowers,

"And I can run away from you, I can!

"Run! run! as fast as you can!

"You can't catch me, I'm the Gingerbread Man!"

"Why," said the fox, "I would not catch you if I could. I would not think of disturbing you."

Just then, the little Gingerbread Boy came to a river. He could not swim across, and he wanted to keep running away from the cow and the horse and the people.

"Jump on my tail, and I will take you across," said the fox.

So the little Gingerbread Boy jumped on the fox's tail, and the fox began to swim the river. When he was a little way from the bank he turned his head, and said, "You are too heavy on my tail, little Gingerbread Boy, I fear I shall let you get wet; jump on my back."

The little Gingerbread Boy jumped on his back.

A little farther out, the fox said, "I am afraid the water will cover you, there; jump on my shoulder."

The little Gingerbread Boy jumped on his shoulder.

In the middle of the stream the fox said, "Oh, dear! little Gingerbread Boy, my shoulder is sinking; jump on my nose, and I can hold you out of water."

So the little Gingerbread Boy jumped on his nose.

The minute the fox reached the bank he threw back his head, and gave a snap!

"Dear me!" said the little Gingerbread Boy, "I am a quarter gone!" The next minute he said, "Why, I am half gone!" The next minute he said, "My goodness gracious, I am three quarters gone!"

And after that, the little Gingerbread Boy never said anything more at all.

THE LITTLE JACKALS AND THE LION[12]

Once there was a great big jungle; and in the jungle there was a great big Lion; and the Lion was king of the jungle. Whenever he wanted anything to eat, all he had to do was to come up out of his cave in the stones and earth and *roar*. When he had roared a few times all the little people of the jungle were so frightened that they came out of their holes and hiding-places and ran, this way and that, to get away. Then, of course, the Lion could see where they were. And he pounced on them, killed them, and gobbled them up.

He did this so often that at last there was not a single thing left alive in the jungle besides the Lion, except two little Jackals,—a little father Jackal and a little mother Jackal.

They had run away so many times that they were quite thin and very tired, and they could not run so fast any more. And one day the Lion was so near that the little mother Jackal grew frightened; she said,—

"Oh, Father Jackal, Father Jackal! I b'lieve our time has come! the Lion will surely catch us this time!"

"Pooh! nonsense, mother!" said the little father Jackal. "Come, we'll run on a bit!"

And they ran, ran, ran very fast, and the Lion did not catch them that time.

But at last a day came when the Lion was nearer still and the little mother Jackal was frightened almost to death.

"Oh, Father Jackal, Father Jackal!" she cried; "I'm sure our time has come! The Lion's going to eat us this time!"

"Now, mother, don't you fret," said the little father Jackal; "you do just as I tell you, and it will be all right."

Then what did those cunning little Jackals do but take hold of hands and run up towards the Lion, as if they had meant to come all the time. When he saw them coming he stood up, and roared in a terrible voice,—

"You miserable little wretches, come here and be eaten, at once! Why didn't you come before?"

The father Jackal bowed very low.

"Indeed, Father Lion," he said, "we meant to come before; we knew we ought to come before; and we wanted to come before; but every time we started to come, a dreadful great lion came out of the woods and roared at us, and frightened us so that we ran away."

"What do you mean?" roared the Lion. "There's no other lion in this jungle, and you know it!"

"Indeed, indeed, Father Lion," said the little Jackal, "I know that is what everybody thinks; but indeed and indeed there is another lion! And he is as much bigger than you as you are bigger than I! His face is much more terrible, and his roar far, far more dreadful. Oh, he is far more fearful than you!"

At that the Lion stood up and roared so that the jungle shook.

"Take me to this Lion," he said; "I'll eat him up and then I'll eat you up."

The little Jackals danced on ahead, and the Lion stalked behind. They led him to a place where there was a round, deep well of clear water. They went round on one side of it, and the Lion stalked up to the other.

"He lives down there, Father Lion!" said the little Jackal. "He lives down there!"

The Lion came close and looked down into the water,—and a lion's face looked back at him out of the water!

When he saw that, the Lion roared and shook his mane and showed his teeth. And the lion in the water shook his mane and showed his teeth. The Lion above shook his mane again and growled again, and made a terrible face. But the lion in the water made just as terrible a one, back. The Lion above couldn't stand that. He leaped down into the well after the other lion.

But, of course, as you know very well, there wasn't any other lion! It was only the reflection in the water!

So the poor old Lion floundered about and floundered about, and as he couldn't get up the steep sides of the well, he was at last drowned. And when he was drowned, the little Jackals took hold of hands and danced round the well, and sang,—

"The Lion is dead! The Lion is dead!

"We have killed the great Lion who would have killed us!

"The Lion is dead! The Lion is dead!

"Ao! Ao! Ao!"

THE COUNTRY MOUSE AND THE CITY MOUSE[13]

Once a little mouse who lived in the country invited a little mouse from the city to visit him. When the little City Mouse sat down to dinner he was surprised to find that the Country Mouse had nothing to eat except barley and grain.

"Really," he said, "you do not live well at all; you should see how I live! I have all sorts of fine things to eat every day. You must come to visit me and see how nice it is to live in the city."

The little Country Mouse was glad to do this, and after a while he went to the city to visit his friend.

The very first place that the City Mouse took the Country Mouse to see was the kitchen cupboard of the house where he lived. There, on the lowest shelf, behind some stone jars, stood a big paper bag of brown sugar. The little City Mouse gnawed a hole in the bag and invited his friend to nibble for himself.

The two little mice nibbled and nibbled, and the Country Mouse thought he had never tasted anything so delicious in his life. He was just thinking how lucky the City Mouse was, when suddenly the door opened with a bang, and in came the cook to get some flour.

"Run!" whispered the City Mouse. And they ran as fast as they could to the little hole where they had come in. The little Country Mouse was shaking all over when they got safely away, but the little City Mouse said, "That is nothing; she will soon go away and then we can go back."

After the cook had gone away and shut the door they stole softly back, and this time the City Mouse had something new to show: he took the little Country Mouse into a corner on the top shelf, where a big jar of dried prunes stood open. After much tugging and pulling they got a large dried prune out of the jar on to the shelf and began to nibble at it. This was even better than the brown sugar. The little Country Mouse liked the taste so much that he could hardly nibble fast enough. But all at once, in the midst of their eating, there came a scratching at the door and a sharp, loud *miaouw*!

"What is that?" said the Country Mouse. The City Mouse just whispered, "Sh!" and ran as fast as he could to the hole. The Country Mouse ran after, you may be sure, as fast as *he* could. As soon as they were out of danger the City Mouse said, "That was the old Cat; she is the best mouser in town,—if she once gets you, you are lost."

"This is very terrible," said the little Country Mouse; "let us not go back to the cupboard again."

"No," said the City Mouse, "I will take you to the cellar; there is something specially fine there."

So the City Mouse took his little friend down the cellar stairs and into a big cupboard where there were many shelves. On the shelves were jars of butter, and cheeses in bags and out of bags. Overhead hung bunches of sausages, and there were spicy apples in barrels standing about. It smelt so good that it went to the little Country Mouse's head. He ran along the shelf and nibbled at a cheese here, and a bit of butter there, until he saw an especially rich, very delicious-smelling piece of cheese on a queer little stand in a corner. He was just on the point of putting his teeth into the cheese when the City Mouse saw him.

"Stop! stop!" cried the City Mouse. "That is a trap!"

The little Country Mouse stopped and said, "What is a trap?"

"That thing is a trap," said the little City Mouse. "The minute you touch the cheese with your teeth something comes down on your head hard, and you're dead."

The little Country Mouse looked at the trap, and he looked at the cheese, and he looked at the little City Mouse. "If you'll excuse me," he said, "I think I will go home. I'd rather have barley and grain to eat and eat it in peace and comfort, than have brown sugar and dried prunes and cheese,— and be frightened to death all the time!"

So the little Country Mouse went back to his home, and there he stayed all the rest of his life.

LITTLE JACK ROLLAROUND[14]

Once upon a time there was a wee little boy who slept in a tiny trundle-bed near his mother's great bed. The trundle-bed had castors on it so that it could be rolled about, and there was nothing in the world the little boy liked so much as to have it rolled. When his mother came to bed he would cry, "Roll me around! roll me around!" And his mother would put out her hand from the big bed and push the little bed back and forth till she was tired. The little boy could never get enough; so for this he was called "Little Jack Rollaround."

One night he had made his mother roll him about, till she fell asleep, and even then he kept crying, "Roll me around! roll me around!" His mother pushed him about in her sleep, until her slumber became too sound; then she stopped. But Little Jack Rollaround kept on crying, "Roll around! roll around!"

By and by the Moon peeped in at the window. He saw a funny sight: Little Jack Rollaround was lying in his trundle-bed, and he had put up one little fat leg for a mast, and fastened the corner of his wee shirt to it for a sail; and he was blowing at it with all his might, and saying, "Roll around! roll around!" Slowly, slowly, the little trundle-bed boat began to move; it sailed along the floor and up the wall and across the ceiling and down again!

"More! more!" cried Little Jack Rollaround; and the little boat sailed faster up the wall, across the ceiling, down the wall, and over the floor. The Moon laughed at the sight; but when Little Jack Rollaround saw the Moon, he called out, "Open the door, old Moon! I want to roll through the town, so that the people can see me!"

The Moon could not open the door, but he shone in through the keyhole, in a broad band. And Little Jack Rollaround sailed his trundle-bed boat up the beam, through the keyhole, and into the street.

"Make a light, old Moon," he said; "I want the people to see me!"

So the good Moon made a light and went along with him, and the little trundle-bed boat went sailing down the streets into the main street of the village. They rolled past the town hall and the schoolhouse and the church; but nobody saw little Jack Rollaround, because everybody was in bed, asleep.

"Why don't the people come to see me?" he shouted.

High up on the church steeple, the Weather-vane answered, "It is no time for people to be in the streets; decent folk are in their beds."

"Then I'll go to the woods, so that the animals may see me," said Little Jack. "Come along, old Moon, and make a light!"

The good Moon went along and made a light, and they came to the forest. "Roll! roll!" cried the little boy; and the trundle-bed went trundling among the trees in the great wood, scaring up the squirrels and startling the little leaves on the trees. The poor old Moon began to have a bad time of it, for the tree-trunks got in his way so that he could not go so fast as the bed, and every time he got behind, the little boy called, "Hurry up, old Moon, I want the beasts to see me!"

But all the animals were asleep, and nobody at all looked at Little Jack Rollaround except an old White Owl; and all she said was, "Who are you?"

The little boy did not like her, so he blew harder, and the trundle-bed boat went sailing through the forest till it came to the end of the world.

"I must go home now; it is late," said the Moon.

"I will go with you; make a path!" said Little Jack Rollaround.

The kind Moon made a path up to the sky, and up sailed the little bed into the midst of the sky. All the little bright Stars were there with their nice little lamps. And when he saw them, that naughty Little Jack Rollaround began to tease. "Out of the way, there! I am coming!" he shouted, and sailed the trundle-bed boat straight at them. He bumped the little Stars right and left, all over the sky, until every one of them put his little lamp out and left it dark.

"Do not treat the little Stars so," said the good Moon.

But Jack Rollaround only behaved the worse: "Get out of the way, old Moon!" he shouted, "I am coming!"

And he steered the little trundle-bed boat straight into the old Moon's face, and bumped his nose!

This was too much for the good Moon; he put out his big light, all at once, and left the sky pitch-black.

"Make a light, old Moon! Make a light!" shouted the little boy. But the Moon answered never a word, and Jack Rollaround could not see where to steer. He went rolling criss-cross, up and down, all over the sky, knocking into the planets and stumbling into the clouds, till he did not know where he was.

Suddenly he saw a big yellow light at the very edge of the sky. He thought it was the Moon. "Look out, I am coming!" he cried, and steered for the light.

But it was not the kind old Moon at all; it was the great mother Sun, just coming up out of her home in the sea, to begin her day's work.

"Aha, youngster, what are you doing in my sky?" she said. And she picked Little Jack Rollaround up and threw him, trundle-bed boat and all, into the middle of the sea!

And I suppose he is there yet, unless somebody picked him out again.

HOW BROTHER RABBIT FOOLED THE WHALE AND THE ELEPHANT[15]

One day little Brother Rabbit was running along on the sand, lippety, lippety, when he saw the Whale and the Elephant talking together. Little Brother Rabbit crouched down and listened to what they were saying. This was what they were saying:—

"You are the biggest thing on the land, Brother Elephant," said the Whale, "and I am the biggest thing in the sea; if we join together we can rule all the animals in the world, and have our way about everything."

"Very good, very good," trumpeted the Elephant; "that suits me; we will do it."

Little Brother Rabbit sniggered to himself. "They won't rule me," he said. He ran away and got a very long, very strong rope, and he got his big drum, and hid the drum a long way off in the bushes. Then he went along the beach till he came to the Whale.

"Oh, please, dear, strong Mr Whale," he said, "will you have the great kindness to do me a favour? My cow is stuck in the mud, a quarter of a mile from here. And I can't pull her out. But you are so strong and so obliging, that I venture to trust you will help me out."

The Whale was so pleased with the compliment that he said, "Yes," at once.

"Then," said the Rabbit, "I will tie this end of my long rope to you, and I will run away and tie the other end round my cow, and when I am ready I will beat my big drum. When you hear that, pull very, very hard, for the cow is stuck very deep in the mud."

"Huh!" grunted the Whale, "I'll pull her out, if she is stuck to the horns."

Little Brother Rabbit tied the rope-end to the Whale, and ran off, lippety, lippety, till he came to the place where the Elephant was.

"Oh, please, mighty and kindly Elephant," he said, making a very low bow, "will you do me a favour?"

"What is it?" asked the Elephant.

"My cow is stuck in the mud, about a quarter of a mile from here," said little Brother Rabbit, "and I cannot pull her out. Of course you could. If you will be so very obliging as to help me——"

"Certainly," said the Elephant grandly, "certainly."

"Then," said little Brother Rabbit, "I will tie one end of this long rope to your trunk, and the other to my cow, and as soon as I have tied her tightly I will beat my big drum. When you hear that, pull; pull as hard as you can, for my cow is very heavy."

"Never fear," said the Elephant, "I could pull twenty cows."

"I am sure you could," said the Rabbit, politely, "only be sure to begin gently, and pull harder and harder till you get her."

Then he tied the end of the rope tightly round the Elephant's trunk, and ran away into the bushes. There he sat down and beat the big drum.

The Whale began to pull, and the Elephant began to pull, and in a jiffy the rope tightened till it was stretched as hard as could be.

"This is a remarkably heavy cow," said the Elephant; "but I'll fetch her!" And he braced his forefeet in the earth, and gave a tremendous pull.

"Dear me!" said the Whale. "That cow must be stuck mighty tight"; and he drove his tail deep in the water, and gave a marvellous pull.

He pulled harder; the Elephant pulled harder. Pretty soon the Whale found himself sliding toward the land. The reason was, of course, that the Elephant had something solid to brace against, and, beside, as fast as he pulled the rope in a little, he took a turn with it round his trunk!

But when the Whale found himself sliding toward the land he was so provoked with the cow that he dived head first, down to the bottom of the sea. That was a pull! The Elephant was jerked off his feet, and came slipping and sliding to the beach, and into the surf. He was terribly angry. He braced himself with all his might, and pulled his best. At the jerk, up came the Whale out of the water.

"Who is pulling me?" spouted the Whale.

"Who is pulling me?" trumpeted the Elephant.

And then each saw the rope in the other's hold.

"I'll teach you to play cow!" roared the Elephant.

"I'll show you how to fool me!" fumed the Whale. And they began to pull again. But this time the rope broke, the Whale turned a somersault, and the Elephant fell over backward.

At that, they were both so ashamed that neither would speak to the other. So that broke up the bargain between them.

And little Brother Rabbit sat in the bushes and laughed, and laughed, and laughed.

THE LITTLE HALF-CHICK

There was once upon a time a Spanish Hen, who hatched out some nice little chickens. She was much pleased with their looks as they came from the shell. One, two, three, came out plump and fluffy; but when the fourth shell broke, out came a little half-chick! It had only one leg and one wing and one eye! It was just half a chicken.

The Hen-mother did not know what in the world to do with the queer little Half-Chick. She was afraid something would happen to it, and she tried hard to protect it and keep it from harm. But as soon as it could walk the little Half-Chick showed a most headstrong spirit, worse than any of its brothers. It would not mind, and it would go wherever it wanted to; it walked with a funny little hoppity-kick, hoppity-kick, and got along pretty fast.

One day the little Half-Chick said, "Mother, I am off to Madrid, to see the King! Good-bye."

The poor Hen-mother did everything she could think of to keep him from doing so foolish a thing, but the little Half-Chick laughed at her naughtily. "I'm for seeing the King," he said; "this life is too quiet for me." And away he went, hoppity-kick, hoppity-kick, over the fields.

When he had gone some distance the little Half-Chick came to a little brook that was caught in the weeds and in much trouble.

"Little Half-Chick," whispered the Water, "I am so choked with these weeds that I cannot move; I am almost lost, for want of room; please push the sticks and weeds away with your bill and help me."

"The idea!" said the little Half-Chick. "I cannot be bothered with you; I am off to Madrid, to see the King!" And in spite of the brook's begging, he went away, hoppity-kick, hoppity-kick.

A bit farther on, the Half-Chick came to a Fire, which was smothered in damp sticks and in great distress.

"Oh, little Half-Chick," said the Fire, "you are just in time to save me. I am almost dead for want of air. Fan me a little with your wing, I beg."

"The idea!" said the little Half-Chick. "I cannot be bothered with you; I am off to Madrid, to see the King!" And he went laughing off, hoppity-kick, hoppity-kick.

When he had hoppity-kicked a good way, and was near Madrid, he came to a clump of bushes, where the Wind was caught fast. The Wind was whimpering, and begging to be set free.

"Little Half-Chick," said the Wind, "you are just in time to help me; if you will brush aside these twigs and leaves, I can get my breath; help me, quickly!"

"Ho! the idea!" said the little Half-Chick "I have no time to bother with you. I am going to Madrid, to see the King." And he went off, hoppity-kick, hoppity-kick, leaving the Wind to smother.

After a while he came to Madrid and to the palace of the King. Hoppity-kick, hoppity-kick, the little Half-Chick skipped past the sentry at the gate, and hoppity-kick, hoppity-kick, he crossed the court. But as he was passing the windows of the kitchen the Cook looked out and saw him.

"The very thing for the King's dinner!" she said. "I was needing a chicken!" And she seized the little Half-Chick by his one wing and threw him into a kettle of water on the fire.

The Water came over the little Half-Chick's feathers, over his head, into his eyes. It was terribly uncomfortable. The little Half-Chick cried out,—

"Water, don't drown me! Stay down, don't come so high!"

"But," the Water said, "Little Half-Chick, little Half-Chick, when I was in trouble you would not help me," and came higher than ever.

Now the Water grew warm, hot, hotter, frightfully hot; the little Half-Chick cried out, "Do not burn so hot, Fire! You are burning me to death! Stop!"

But the Fire said, "Little Half-Chick, little Half-Chick, when I was in trouble you would not help me," and burned hotter than ever.

Just as the little Half-Chick thought he must suffocate, the Cook took the cover off, to look at the dinner. "Dear me," she said, "this chicken is no good; it is burned to a cinder." And she picked the little Half-Chick up by one leg and threw him out of the window.

In the air he was caught by a breeze and taken up higher than the trees. Round and round he was twirled till he was so dizzy he thought he must perish. "Don't blow me so, Wind," he cried, "let me down!"

"Little Half-Chick, little Half-Chick," said the Wind, "when I was in trouble you would not help me!" And the Wind blew him straight up to the top of the church steeple, and stuck him there, fast!

There he stands to this day, with his one eye, his one wing, and his one leg. He cannot hoppity-kick any more, but he turns slowly round when the wind blows, and keeps his head toward it, to hear what it says.

THE BLACKBERRY-BUSH[16]

A little boy sat at his mother's knees, by the long western window, looking out into the garden. It was autumn, and the wind was sad; and the golden elm leaves lay scattered about among the grass, and on the gravel path. The mother was knitting a little stocking; her fingers moved the bright needles; but her eyes were fixed on the clear evening sky.

As the darkness gathered, the wee boy laid his head on her lap and kept so still that, at last, she leaned forward to look into his dear round face. He was not asleep, but was watching very earnestly a blackberry-bush, that waved its one tall, dark-red spray in the wind outside the fence.

"What are you thinking about, my darling?" she said, smoothing his soft, honey-coloured hair.

"The blackberry-bush, mamma; what does it say? It keeps nodding, nodding to me behind the fence; what does it say, mamma?"

"It says," she answered, "'I see a happy little boy in the warm, fire-lighted room. The wind blows cold, and here it is dark and lonely; but that little boy is warm and happy and safe at his mother's knees. I nod to him, and he looks at me. I wonder if he knows how happy he is!

"'See, all my leaves are dark crimson. Every day they dry and wither more and more; by and by they will be so weak they can scarcely cling to my branches, and the north wind will tear them all away, and nobody will remember them any more. Then the snow will sink down and wrap me close. Then the snow will melt again and icy rain will clothe me, and the bitter wind will rattle my bare twigs up and down.

"'I nod my head to all who pass, and dreary nights and dreary days go by; but in the happy house, so warm and bright, the little boy plays all day with books and toys. His mother and his father cherish him; he nestles on their knees in the red firelight at night, while they read to him lovely stories, or sing sweet old songs to him,—the happy little boy! And outside I peep over the snow and see a stream of ruddy light from a crack in the window-shutter, and I nod out here alone in the dark, thinking how beautiful it is.

"'And here I wait patiently. I take the snow and the rain and the cold, and I am not sorry, but glad; for in my roots I feel warmth and life, and I know that a store of greenness and beauty is shut up safe in my small brown buds. Day and night go again and again; little by little the snow melts all away; the ground grows soft; the sky is blue; the little birds fly over, crying, "It is spring! it is spring!" Ah! then through all my twigs I feel the slow sap stirring.

"'Warmer grow the sunbeams, and softer the air. The small blades of grass creep thick about my feet; the sweet rain helps to swell my shining buds. More and more I push forth my leaves, till out I burst in a gay green dress, and nod in joy and pride. The little boy comes running to look at me, and cries, "Oh, mamma! the little blackberry-bush is alive and beautiful and green. Oh, come and see!" And I hear; and I bow my head in the summer wind; and every day they watch me grow more beautiful, till at last I shake out blossoms, fair and fragrant.

"'A few days more, and I drop the white petals down among the grass, and, lo! there are the green tiny berries! Carefully I hold them up to the sun; carefully I gather the dew in the summer nights; slowly they ripen; they grow larger and redder and darker, and at last they are black, shining, delicious. I hold them as high as I can for the little boy, who comes dancing out. He shouts with joy, and gathers them in his dear hand; and he runs to share them with his mother, saying, "Here is what the patient blackberry-bush bore for us: see how nice, mamma!"

"'Ah! then indeed I am glad, and would say, if I could, "Yes, take them, dear little boy; I kept them for you, held them long up to the sun and rain to make them sweet and ripe for you"; and I nod and nod in full content, for my work is done. From the window he watches me and thinks, "There is the little blackberry-bush that was so kind to me. I see it and I love it. I know it is safe out there nodding all alone, and next summer it will hold ripe berries up for me to gather again."'"

Then the wee boy smiled, and said he liked the little story. His mother took him up in her arms, and they went out to supper and left the blackberry-bush nodding up and down in the wind; and there it is nodding yet.

THE FAIRIES[17]

Up the airy mountain,
	Down the rushy glen,
We daren't go a-hunting
	For fear of little men.
Wee folk, good folk,
	Trooping all together;
Green jacket, red cap,
	And white owl's feather!

Down along the rocky shore
	Some make their home—
They live on crispy pancakes
	Of yellow tide-foam;
Some in the reeds
	Of the black mountain-lake,
With frogs for their watch-dogs,
	All night awake.

High on the hilltop
	The old King sits;
He is now so old and gray,
	He's nigh lost his wits.
With a bridge of white mist
	Columbkill he crosses,
On his stately journeys
	From Slieveleague to Rosses;
Or going up with music
	On cold starry nights,
To sup with the Queen
	Of the gay Northern Lights.

They stole little Bridget

For seven years long;
When she came down again
    Her friends were all gone.
They took her lightly back,
    Between the night and morrow;
They thought that she was fast asleep,
    But she was dead with sorrow.
They have kept her ever since
    Deep within the lake,
On a bed of flag-leaves,
    Watching till she wake.

By the craggy hillside,
    Through the mosses bare,
They have planted thorn-trees,
    For pleasure here and there.
Is any man so daring
    As dig them up in spite,
He shall find their sharpest thorns
    In his bed at night.

Up the airy mountain,
    Down the rushy glen,
We daren't go a-hunting
    For fear of little men.
Wee folk, good folk,
    Trooping all together;
Green jacket, red cap,
    And white owl's feather!

THE ADVENTURES OF THE LITTLE FIELD MOUSE

Once upon a time, there was a little brown Field Mouse; and one day he was out in the fields to see what he could find. He was running along in the grass, poking his nose into everything and looking with his two eyes all about, when he saw a smooth, shiny acorn, lying in the grass. It was such a fine shiny little acorn that he thought he would take it home with him; so he put out his paw to touch it, but the little acorn rolled away from him. He ran after it, but it kept rolling on, just ahead of him, till it came to a place where a big oak-tree had its roots spread all over the ground. Then it rolled under a big round root.

Little Mr Field Mouse ran to the root and poked his nose under after the acorn, and there he saw a small round hole in the ground. He slipped through and saw some stairs going down into the earth. The acorn was rolling down, with a soft tapping sound, ahead of him, so down he went too. Down, down, down, rolled the acorn, and down, down, down, went the Field Mouse, until suddenly he saw a tiny door at the foot of the stairs.

The shiny acorn rolled to the door and struck against it with a tap. Quickly the little door opened and the acorn rolled inside. The Field Mouse hurried as fast as he could down the last stairs, and pushed through just as the door was closing. It shut behind him, and he was in a little room. And there, before him, stood a queer little Red Man! He had a little red cap, and a little red jacket, and odd little red shoes with points at the toes.

"You are my prisoner," he said to the Field Mouse.

"What for?" said the Field Mouse.

"Because you tried to steal my acorn," said the little Red Man.

"It is my acorn," said the Field Mouse; "I found it."

"No, it isn't," said the little Red Man, "I have it; you will never see it again."

The little Field Mouse looked all about the room as fast as he could, but he could not see any acorn. Then he thought he would go back up the tiny stairs to his own home. But the little door was locked, and the little Red Man had the key. And he said to the poor mouse,—

"You shall be my servant; you shall make my bed and sweep my room and cook my broth."

So the little brown Mouse was the little Red Man's servant, and every day he made the little Red Man's bed and swept the little Red Man's room and cooked the little Red Man's broth. And every day the little Red Man went away through the tiny door, and did not come back till afternoon. But he always locked the door after him, and carried away the key.

At last, one day he was in such a hurry that he turned the key before the door was quite latched, which, of course, didn't lock it at all. He went away without noticing,—he was in such a hurry.

The little Field Mouse knew that his chance had come to run away home. But he didn't want to go without the pretty, shiny acorn. Where it was he didn't know, so he looked everywhere. He opened every little drawer and looked in, but it wasn't in any of the drawers; he peeped on every shelf, but it wasn't on a shelf; he hunted in every closet, but it wasn't in there. Finally, he climbed up on a chair and opened a wee, wee door in the chimney-piece, —and there it was!

He took it quickly in his forepaws, and then he took it in his mouth, and then he ran away. He pushed open the little door; he climbed up, up, up the little stairs; he came out through the hole under the root; he ran and ran through the fields; and at last he came to his own house.

When he was in his own house he set the shiny acorn on the table. I expect he set it down hard, for all at once, with a little snap, it opened!— exactly like a little box.

And what do you think! There was a tiny necklace inside! It was a most beautiful tiny necklace, all made of jewels, and it was just big enough for a lady mouse. So the little Field Mouse gave the tiny necklace to his little Mouse-sister. She thought it was perfectly lovely. And when she wasn't wearing it she kept it in the shiny acorn box.

And the little Red Man never knew what had become of it, because he didn't know where the little Field Mouse lived.

ANOTHER LITTLE RED HEN[18]

Once upon a time there was a little Red Hen, who lived on a farm all by herself. An old Fox, crafty and sly, had a den in the rocks, on a hill near her house. Many and many a night this old Fox used to lie awake and think to himself how good that little Red Hen would taste if he could once get her in his big kettle and boil her for dinner. But he couldn't catch the little Red Hen, because she was too wise for him. Every time she went out to market she locked the door of the house behind her, and as soon as she came in again she locked the door behind her and put the key in her apron pocket, where she kept her scissors and some sugar candy.

At last the old Fox thought out a way to catch the little Red Hen. Early in the morning he said to his old mother, "Have the kettle boiling when I come home to-night, for I'll be bringing the little Red Hen for supper." Then he took a big bag and slung it over his shoulder, and walked till he came to the little Red Hen's house. The little Red Hen was just coming out of her door to pick up a few sticks for firewood. So the old Fox hid behind the wood-pile, and as soon as she bent down to get a stick, into the house he slipped, and scurried behind the door.

In a minute the little Red Hen came quickly in, and shut the door and locked it. "I'm glad I'm safely in," she said. Just as she said it, she turned round, and there stood the ugly old Fox, with his big bag over his shoulder. Whiff! how scared the little Red Hen was! She dropped her apronful of sticks, and flew up to the big beam across the ceiling. There she perched, and she said to the old Fox, down below, "You may as well go home, for you can't get me."

"Can't I, though!" said the Fox. And what do you think he did? He stood on the floor underneath the little Red Hen and twirled round in a circle after his own tail. And as he spun, and spun, and spun, faster, and faster, and faster, the poor little Red Hen got so dizzy watching him that she couldn't hold on to the perch. She dropped off, and the old Fox picked her up and put her in his bag, slung the bag over his shoulder, and started for home, where the kettle was boiling.

He had a very long way to go, up hill, and the little Red Hen was still so dizzy that she didn't know where she was. But when the dizziness began to go off, she whisked her little scissors out of her apron pocket, and snip! she cut a little hole in the bag; then she poked her head out and saw where she was, and as soon as they came to a good spot she cut the hole bigger and jumped out herself. There was a great big stone lying there, and the little Red Hen picked it up and put it in the bag as quick as a wink. Then she ran as fast as she could till she came to her own little farmhouse, and she went in and locked the door with the big key.

The old Fox went on carrying the stone and never knew the difference. My, but it bumped him well! He was pretty tired when he got home. But he was so pleased to think of the supper he was going to have that he did not mind that at all. As soon as his mother opened the door he said, "Is the kettle boiling?"

"Yes," said his mother; "have you got the little Red Hen?"

"I have," said the old Fox. "When I open the bag you hold the cover off the kettle and I'll shake the bag so that the Hen will fall in, and then you pop the cover on, before she can jump out."

"All right," said his mean old mother; and she stood close by the boiling kettle, ready to put the cover on.

The Fox lifted the big, heavy bag up till it was over the open kettle, and gave it a shake. Splash! thump! splash! In went the stone and out came the boiling water, all over the old Fox and the old Fox's mother!

And they were scalded to death.

But the little Red Hen lived happily ever after, in her own little farmhouse.

THE STORY OF THE LITTLE RID HIN

There was once't upon a time
    A little small Rid Hin,
Off in the good ould country
    Where yees ha' nivir bin.

Nice and quiet shure she was,
    And nivir did any harrum;
She lived alane all be herself,
    And worked upon her farrum.

There lived out o'er the hill,
    In a great din o' rocks,
A crafty, shly, and wicked
    Ould folly iv a Fox.

This rashkill iv a Fox,
    He tuk it in his head
He'd have the little Rid Hin:
    So, whin he wint to bed,

He laid awake and thaught
    What a foine thing 'twad be
To fetch her home and bile her up
    For his ould marm and he.

And so he thaught and thaught,
    Until he grew so thin
That there was nothin' left of him

But jist his bones and shkin.

But the small Rid Hin was wise,
    She always locked her door,
And in her pocket pit the key,
    To keep the Fox out shure.

But at last there came a schame
    Intil his wicked head,
And he tuk a great big bag
    And to his mither said,—

"Now have the pot all bilin'
    Agin the time I come;
We'll ate the small Rid Hin to-night,
    For shure I'll bring her home."

And so away he wint
    Wid the bag upon his back,
An' up the hill and through the woods
    Saftly he made his track.

An' thin he came alang,
    Craping as shtill's a mouse,
To where the little small Rid Hin
    Lived in her shnug ould house.

An' out she comes hersel',
    Jist as he got in sight,
To pick up shticks to make her fire:
    "Aha!" says Fox, "all right.

"Begorra, now, I'll have yees
    Widout much throuble more";
An' in he shlips quite unbeknownst,
    An' hides be'ind the door.

An' thin, a minute afther,
    In comes the small Rid Hin,
An' shuts the door, and locks it, too,
    An' thinks, "I'm safely in."

An' thin she tarns around
    An' looks be'ind the door;
There shtands the Fox wid his big tail
    Shpread out upon the floor.

Dear me! she was so schared
    Wid such a wondrous sight,
She dropped her apronful of shticks,
    An' flew up in a fright,

An' lighted on the bame
    Across on top the room;
"Aha!" says she, "ye don't have me;
    Ye may as well go home."

"Aha!" says Fox, "we'll see;
    I'll bring yees down from that."
So out he marched upon the floor
    Right under where she sat.

An' thin he whiruled around,
    An' round an' round an' round,

Fashter an' fashter an' fashter,
        Afther his tail on the ground.

Until the small Rid Hin
        She got so dizzy, shure,
Wid lookin' at the Fox's tail,
        She jist dropped on the floor.

An' Fox he whipped her up,
        An' pit her in his bag,
An' off he started all alone,
        Him and his little dag.

All day he tracked the wood
        Up hill an' down again;
An' wid him, shmotherin' in the bag,
        The little small Rid Hin.

Sorra a know she knowed
        Awhere she was that day;
Says she, "I'm biled an' ate up, shure
        An' what'll be to pay?"

Thin she betho't hersel',
        An' tuk her schissors out,
An' shnipped a big hole in the bag,
        So she could look about.

An' 'fore ould Fox could think
        She lept right out—she did,
An' thin picked up a great big shtone,
        An' popped it in instid.

An' thin she rins off home,
      Her outside door she locks;
Thinks she, "You see you don't have me,
      You crafty, shly ould Fox."

An' Fox he tugged away
      Wid the great big hivy shtone,
Thimpin' his shoulders very bad
      As he wint in alone.

An' whin he came in sight
      O' his great din o' rocks,
Jist watchin' for him at the door
      He shpied ould mither Fox.

"Have ye the pot a-bilin'?"
      Says he to ould Fox thin;
"Shure an' it is, me child," says she;
      "Have ye the small Rid Hin?"

"Yes, jist here in me bag,
      As shure as I shtand here;
Open the lid till I pit her in:
      Open it—nivir fear."

So the rashkill cut the shtring,
      An' hild the big bag over;
"Now when I shake it in," says he,
      "Do ye pit on the cover."

"Yis, that I will"; an' thin

The shtone wint in wid a dash,
An' the pot o' bilin' wather
    Came over them ker-splash.

An' schalted 'em both to death,
    So they couldn't brathe no more;
An' the little small Rid Hin lived safe,
    Jist where she lived before.

THE STORY OF EPAMINONDAS AND HIS AUNTIE[19]

Epaminondas used to go to see his Auntie 'most every day, and she nearly always gave him something to take home to his Mammy.

One day she gave him a big piece of cake; nice, yellow, rich gold-cake.

Epaminondas took it in his fist and held it all crunched up tight, like this, and came along home. By the time he got home there wasn't anything left but a fistful of crumbs. His Mammy said,—

"What you got there, Epaminondas?"

"Cake, Mammy," said Epaminondas.

"Cake!" said his Mammy. "Epaminondas, you ain't got the sense you was born with! That's no way to carry cake. The way to carry cake is to wrap it all up nice in some leaves and put it in your hat, and put your hat on your head, and come along home. You hear me, Epaminondas?"

"Yes, Mammy," said Epaminondas.

Next day Epaminondas went to see his Auntie, and she gave him a pound of butter for his Mammy; fine, fresh, sweet butter.

Epaminondas wrapped it up in leaves and put it in his hat, and put his hat on his head, and came along home. It was a very hot day. Pretty soon the butter began to melt. It melted, and melted, and as it melted it ran down Epaminondas' forehead; then it ran over his face, and in his ears, and down his neck. When he got home, all the butter Epaminondas had was *on him*. His Mammy looked at him, and then she said,—

"Law's sake! Epaminondas, what you got in your hat?"

"Butter, Mammy," said Epaminondas; "Auntie gave it to me."

"Butter!" said his Mammy. "Epaminondas, you ain't got the sense you was born with! Don't you know that's no way to carry butter? The way to carry butter is to wrap it up in some leaves and take it down to the brook, and cool it in the water, and cool it in the water, and cool it in the water, and then take it on your hands, careful, and bring it along home."

"Yes, Mammy," said Epaminondas.

By and by, another day, Epaminondas went to see his Auntie again, and; this time she gave him a little new puppy-dog to take home.

Epaminondas put it in some leaves and took it down to the brook; and there he cooled it in the water, and cooled it in the water, and cooled it in the water; then he took it in his hands and came along home. When he got home, the puppy-dog was dead. His Mammy looked at it, and she said,—

"Law's sake! Epaminondas, what you got there?"

"A puppy-dog, Mammy," said Epaminondas.

"A *puppy-dog*!" said his Mammy. "My gracious sakes alive, Epaminondas, you ain't got the sense you was born with! That ain't the way to carry a puppy-dog! The way to carry a puppy-dog is to take a long piece of string and tie one end of it round the puppy-dog's neck and put the puppy-dog on the ground, and take hold of the other end of the string and come along home, like this."

"All right, Mammy," said Epaminondas.

Next day Epaminondas went to see his Auntie again, and when he came to go home she gave him a loaf of bread to carry to his Mammy; a brown, fresh, crusty loaf of bread.

So Epaminondas tied a string around the end of the loaf and took hold of the end of the string and came along home, like this. (Imitate dragging something along the ground.) When he got home his Mammy looked at the thing on the end of the string, and she said,—

"My laws a-massy! Epaminondas, what you got on the end of that string?"

"Bread, Mammy," said Epaminondas; "Auntie gave it to me."

"Bread!!!" said his Mammy. "O Epaminondas, Epaminondas, you ain't got the sense you was born with; you never did have the sense you was born with; you never will have the sense you was born with! Now I ain't gwine tell you any more ways to bring truck home. And don't you go see your Auntie, neither. I'll go see her my own self. But I'll just tell you one thing, Epaminondas! You see these here six mince pies I done make? You see how I done set 'em on the doorstep to cool? Well, now, you hear me, Epaminondas, *you be careful how you step on those pies!*"

"Yes, Mammy," said Epaminondas.

Then Epaminondas' Mammy put on her bonnet and her shawl and took a basket in her hand and went away to see Auntie. The six mince pies sat cooling in a row on the doorstep.

And then,—and then,—Epaminondas *was* careful how he stepped on those pies!

He stepped (imitate)—right—in—the—middle—of—every—one.

And, do you know, children, nobody knows what happened next! The person who told me the story didn't know; nobody knows. But you can guess.

THE BOY WHO CRIED "WOLF!"

There was once a shepherd-boy who kept his flock at a little distance from the village. Once he thought he would play a trick on the villagers and have some fun at their expense. So he ran toward the village crying out, with all his might,—

"Wolf! Wolf! Come and help! The wolves are at my lambs!"

The kind villagers left their work and ran to the field to help him. But when they got there the boy laughed at them for their pains; there was no wolf there.

Still another day the boy tried the same trick, and the villagers came running to help and got laughed at again.

Then one day a wolf did break into the fold and began killing the lambs. In great fright, the boy ran for help. "Wolf! Wolf!" he screamed. "There is a wolf in the flock! Help!"

The villagers heard him, but they thought it was another mean trick; no one paid the least attention, or went near him. And the shepherd-boy lost all his sheep.

That is the kind of thing that happens to people who lie: even when they tell the truth no one believes them.

THE FROG KING

Did you ever hear the old story about the foolish Frogs? The Frogs in a certain swamp decided that they needed a king; they had always got along perfectly well without one, but they suddenly made up their minds that a king they must have. They sent a messenger to Jove and begged him to send a king to rule over them.

Jove saw how stupid they were, and sent a king who could not harm them: he tossed a big log into the middle of the pond.

At the splash the Frogs were terribly frightened, and dived into their holes to hide from King Log. But after a while, when they saw that the king never moved, they got over their fright and went and sat on him. And as soon as they found he really could not hurt them they began to despise him; and finally they sent another messenger to Jove to ask for a new king.

Jove sent an eel.

The Frogs were much pleased and a good deal frightened when King Eel came wriggling and swimming among them. But as the days went on, and the eel was perfectly harmless, they stopped being afraid; and as soon as they stopped fearing King Eel they stopped respecting him.

Soon they sent a third messenger to Jove, and begged that they might have a better king,—a king who was worth while.

It was too much; Jove was angry at their stupidity at last. "I will give you a king such as you deserve!" he said; and he sent them a Stork.

As soon as the Frogs came to the surface to greet the new king, King Stork caught them in his long bill and gobbled them up. One after another they came bobbing up, and one after another the stork ate them. He was indeed a king worthy of them!

THE SUN AND THE WIND

The Sun and the Wind once had a quarrel as to which was the stronger. Each believed himself to be the more powerful. While they were arguing they saw a traveller walking along the country highway, wearing a great cloak.

"Here is a chance to test our strength," said the Wind; "let us see which of us is strong enough to make that traveller take off his cloak; the one who can do that shall be acknowledged the more powerful."

"Agreed," said the Sun.

Instantly the Wind began to blow; he puffed and tugged at the man's cloak, and raised a storm of hail and rain, to beat at it. But the colder it grew and the more it stormed, the tighter the traveller held his cloak around him. The Wind could not get it off.

Now it was the Sun's turn. He shone with all his beams on the man's shoulders. As it grew hotter and hotter, the man unfastened his cloak; then he threw it back; at last he took it off! The Sun had won.

THE LITTLE JACKAL AND THE ALLIGATOR

The little Jackal was very fond of shell-fish. He used to go down by the river and hunt along the edges for crabs and such things. And once, when he was hunting for crabs, he was so hungry that he put his paw into the water after a crab without looking first,—which you never should do! The minute he put in his paw, *snap!*—the big Alligator who lives in the mud down there had it in his jaws.

"Oh, dear!" thought the little Jackal; "the big Alligator has my paw in his mouth! In another minute he will pull me down and gobble me up! What shall I do? what shall I do?" Then he thought, suddenly, "I'll deceive him!"

So he put on a very cheerful voice, as if nothing at all were the matter, and he said,—

"Ho! ho! Clever Mr Alligator! Smart Mr Alligator, to take that old bulrush root for my paw! I hope you'll find it very tender!"

The old Alligator was hidden away beneath the mud and bulrush leaves, and he couldn't see anything. He thought, "Pshaw! I've made a mistake." So he opened his mouth and let the little Jackal go.

The little Jackal ran away as fast as he could, and as he ran he called out,—

"Thank you, Mr Alligator! Kind Mr Alligator! *So* kind of you to let me go!"

The old Alligator lashed with his tail and snapped with his jaws, but it was too late; the little Jackal was out of reach.

After this the little Jackal kept away from the river, out of danger. But after about a week he got such an appetite for crabs that nothing else would do at all; he felt that he must have a crab. So he went down by the river and looked all around, very carefully. He didn't see the old Alligator, but he thought to himself, "I think I'll not take any chances." So he stood still and began to talk out loud to himself. He said,—

"When I don't see any little crabs on the land I generally see them sticking out of the water, and then I put my paw in and catch them. I wonder if there are any fat little crabs in the water to-day?"

The old Alligator was hidden down in the mud at the bottom of the river, and when he heard what the little Jackal said, he thought, "Aha! I'll pretend to be a little crab, and when he puts his paw in, I'll make my dinner of him." So he stuck the black end of his snout above the water and waited.

The little Jackal took one look, and then he said,—

"Thank you, Mr Alligator! Kind Mr Alligator! You are *exceedingly* kind to show me where you are! I will have dinner elsewhere." And he ran away like the wind.

The old Alligator foamed at the mouth, he was so angry, but the little Jackal was gone.

For two whole weeks the little Jackal kept away from the river. Then, one day he got a feeling inside him that nothing but crabs could satisfy: he felt that he must have at least one crab. Very cautiously, he went down to the river and looked all around. He saw no sign of the old Alligator. Still, he did not mean to take any chances. So he stood quite still and began to talk to himself,—it was a little way he had. He said,—

"When I don't see any little crabs on the shore, or sticking up out of the water, I usually see them blowing bubbles from under the water; the little bubbles go *puff, puff, puff,* and then they go *pop, pop, pop,* and they show me where the little juicy crabs are, so I can put my paw in and catch them. I wonder if I shall see any little bubbles to-day?"

The old Alligator, lying low in the mud and weeds, heard this, and he thought, "Pooh! *That's* easy enough; I'll just blow some little crab-bubbles, and then he will put his paw in where I can get it."

So he blew, and he blew, a mighty blast, and the bubbles rose in a perfect whirlpool, fizzing and swirling.

The little Jackal didn't have to be told who was underneath those bubbles: he took one quick look, and off he ran. But as he went, he sang,—

"Thank you, Mr Alligator! Kind Mr Alligator! You are the kindest Alligator in the world, to show me where you are, so nicely! I'll breakfast at another part of the river."

The old Alligator was so furious that he crawled up on the bank and went after the little Jackal; but, dear, dear, he couldn't catch the little Jackal; he ran far too fast.

After this, the little Jackal did not like to risk going near the water, so he ate no more crabs. But he found a garden of wild figs, which were so good that he went there every day, and ate them instead of shell-fish.

Now the old Alligator found this out, and he made up his mind to have the little Jackal for supper, or to die trying. So he crept, and crawled, and dragged himself over the ground to the garden of wild figs. There he made a huge pile of figs under the biggest of the wild fig trees, and hid himself in the pile.

After a while the little Jackal came dancing into the garden, very happy and free from care,—*but* looking all around. He saw the huge pile of figs under the big fig tree.

"H-m," he thought, "that looks singularly like my friend, the Alligator. I'll investigate a bit."

He stood quite still and began to talk to himself,—it was a little way he had. He said,—

"The little figs I like best are the fat, ripe, juicy ones that drop off when the breeze blows; and then the wind blows them about on the ground, this way and that; the great heap of figs over there is so still that I think they must be all bad figs."

The old Alligator, underneath his fig pile, thought,—

"Bother the suspicious little Jackal! I shall have to make these figs roll about, so that he will think the wind moves them." And straight-way he humped himself up and moved, and sent the little figs flying,—and his back showed through.

The little Jackal did not wait for a second look. He ran out of the garden like the wind. But as he ran he called back,—

"Thank you, again, Mr Alligator; very sweet of you to show me where you are; I can't stay to thank you as I should like: good-bye!"

At this the old Alligator was beside himself with rage. He vowed that he would have the little Jackal for supper this time, come what might. So he crept and crawled over the ground till he came to the little Jackal's house. Then he crept and crawled inside, and hid himself there in the house, to wait till the little Jackal should come home.

By and by the little Jackal came dancing home, happy and free from care,—*but* looking all around. Presently, as he came along, he saw that the ground was all raked up as if something very heavy had been dragged over it. The little Jackal stopped and looked.

"What's this? what's this?" he said.

Then he saw that the door of his house was crushed at the sides and broken, as if something very big had gone through it.

"What's this? What's this?" the little Jackal said. "I think I'll investigate a little!"

So he stood quite still and began to talk to himself (you remember, it was a little way he had), but loudly. He said,—

"How strange that my little House doesn't speak to me! Why don't you speak to me, little House? You always speak to me, if everything is all right, when I come home. I wonder if anything is wrong with my little House?"

The old Alligator thought to himself that he must certainly pretend to be the little House, or the little Jackal would never come in. So he put on as pleasant a voice as he could (which is not saying much) and said,—

"Hullo, little Jackal!"

Oh! When the little Jackal heard that, he was frightened enough, for once.

"It's the old Alligator," he said, "and if I don't make an end of him this time he will certainly make an end of me. What shall I do?"

He thought very fast. Then he spoke out pleasantly.

"Thank you, little House," he said, "it's good to hear your pretty voice, dear little House, and I will be in with you in a minute; only first I must gather some firewood for dinner."

Then he went and gathered firewood, and more firewood, and more firewood; and he piled it all up solid against the door and round the house; and then he set fire to it!

And it smoked and burned till it smoked that old Alligator to smoked herring!

THE LARKS IN THE CORNFIELD

There was once a family of little Larks who lived with their mother in a nest in a cornfield. When the corn was ripe the mother Lark watched very carefully to see if there were any sign of the reapers' coming, for she knew that when they came their sharp knives would cut down the nest and hurt the baby Larks. So every day, when she went out for food, she told the little Larks to look and listen very closely to everything that went on, and to tell her all they saw and heard when she came home.

One day when she came home the little Larks were much frightened.

"Oh, Mother, dear Mother," they said, "you must move us away to-night! The farmer was in the field to-day, and he said, 'The corn is ready to cut; we must call in the neighbours to help.' And then he told his son to go out to-night and ask all the neighbours to come and reap the corn to-morrow."

The mother Lark laughed. "Don't be frightened," she said; "if he waits for his neighbours to reap the corn we shall have plenty of time to move; tell me what he says to-morrow."

The next night the little Larks were quite trembling with fear; the moment their mother got home they cried out, "Mother, you must surely move us to-night! The farmer came to-day and said, 'The corn is getting too ripe; we cannot wait for our neighbours; we must ask our relatives to help us.' And then he called his son and told him to ask all the uncles and cousins to come to-morrow and cut the corn. Shall we not move to-night?"

"Don't worry," said the mother Lark; "the uncles and cousins have plenty of reaping to do for themselves; we'll not move yet."

The third night, when the mother Lark came home, the baby Larks said, "Mother, dear, the farmer came to the field to-day, and when he looked at the corn he was quite angry; he said, 'This will never do! The corn is getting too ripe; it's no use to wait for our relatives, we shall have to cut this corn ourselves.' And then he called his son and said, 'Go out to-night and hire reapers, and to-morrow we will begin to cut.'"

"Well," said the mother, "that is another story; when a man begins to do his own business, instead of asking somebody else to do it, things get done. I will move you out to-night."

A TRUE STORY ABOUT A GIRL

Once there were four little girls who lived in a big, bare house, in the country. They were very poor, but they had the happiest times you ever heard of, because they were very rich in everything except money. They had a wonderful, wise father, who knew stories to tell, and who taught them their lessons in such a beautiful way that it was better than play; they had a lovely, merry, kind mother, who was never too tired to help them work or watch them play; and they had all the great green country to play in. There were dark, shadowy woods, and fields of flowers, and a river. And there was a big barn.

One of the little girls was named Louisa. She was very pretty, and ever so strong; she could run for miles through the woods and not get tired. She had a splendid brain in her little head; it liked study, and it thought interesting thoughts all day long.

Louisa liked to sit in a corner by herself, sometimes, and write thoughts in her diary; all the little girls kept diaries. She liked to make up stories out of her own head, and sometimes she made verses.

When the four little sisters had finished their lessons, and had helped their mother wash up and sew, they used to go to the big barn to play; and the best play of all was theatricals. Louisa liked theatricals better than anything.

They made the barn into a theatre, and the grown-up people came to see the plays they acted. They used to climb up on the hay-loft for a stage, and the grown people sat in chairs on the floor. It was great fun. One of the plays they acted was *Jack and the Beanstalk*. They had a ladder from the floor to the loft, and on the ladder they tied a vine all the way up to the loft, to look like the wonderful beanstalk. One of the little girls was dressed up to look like Jack, and she acted that part. When it came to the place in the story where the giant tried to follow Jack, the little girl cut down the beanstalk, and down came the giant tumbling from the loft. The giant was made out of pillows, with a great, fierce head of paper, and funny clothes.

Another story that they acted was *Cinderella*. They made a wonderful big pumpkin out of the wheelbarrow, trimmed with yellow paper, and Cinderella rolled away in it, when the fairy godmother waved her wand.

One other beautiful story they used to play. It was the story of *Pilgrim's Progress*; if you have never heard it, you must be sure to read it as soon as you can read well enough to understand the old-fashioned words. The little girls used to put shells in their hats for a sign they were on a pilgrimage, as the old pilgrims used to do; then they made journeys over the hill behind the house, and through the woods, and down the lanes; and when the pilgrimage was over they had apples and nuts to eat, in the happy land of home.

Louisa loved all these plays, and she made some of her own and wrote them down so that the children could act them.

But better than fun or writing Louisa loved her mother, and by and by, as the little girl began to grow into a big girl, she felt very sad to see her dear mother work so hard. She helped all she could with the housework, but nothing could really help the tired mother except money; she needed money for food and clothes, and someone grown up, to help in the house. But there never was enough money for these things, and Louisa's mother grew more and more weary, and sometimes ill. I cannot tell you how much Louisa suffered over this.

At last, as Louisa thought about it, she came to care more about helping her mother and her father and her sisters than about anything else in all the world. And she began to work very hard to earn money. She sewed for people, and when she was a little older she taught some little girls their lessons, and then she wrote stories for the papers. Every bit of money she earned, except what she had to use, she gave to her dear family. It helped very much, but it was so little that Louisa never felt as if she were doing anything.

Every year she grew more unselfish, and every year she worked harder. She liked writing stories best of all her work, but she did not get much money for them, and some people told her she was wasting her time.

At last, one day, a publisher asked Louisa, who was now a woman, to write a book for girls. Louisa was not very well, and she was very tired, but she always said, "I'll try," when she had a chance to work; so she said, "I'll try," to the publisher. When she thought about the book she remembered the good times she used to have with her sisters in the big, bare house in the country. And so she wrote a story and put all that in it; she put her dear mother and her wise father in it, and all the little sisters, and besides the jolly times and the plays, she put the sad, hard times in,—the work and worry and going without things.

When the book was written, she called it *Little Women,* and sent it to the publisher.

And, children, the little book made Louisa famous. It was so sweet and funny and sad and real,—like our own lives,—that everybody wanted to read it. Everybody bought it, and much money came from it. After so many years, little Louisa's wish came true: she bought a nice house for her family; she sent one of her sisters to Europe, to study; she gave her father books; but best of all, she was able to see to it that the beloved mother, so tired and so ill, could have rest and happiness. Never again did the dear mother have to do any hard work, and she had pretty things about her all the rest of her life.

Louisa Alcott, for that was Louisa's name, wrote many beautiful books after this, and she became one of the most famous women of America. But I think the most beautiful thing about her is what I have been telling you: that she loved her mother so well that she gave her whole life to make her happy.

MY KINGDOM

The little Louisa I told you about, who wrote verses and stories in her diary, used to like to play that she was a princess, and that her kingdom was her own mind. When she had unkind or dissatisfied thoughts, she tried to get rid of them by playing they were enemies of the kingdom; and she drove them out with soldiers; the soldiers were patience, duty, and love. It used to help Louisa to be good to play this, and I think it may have helped make her the splendid woman she was afterward. Maybe you would like to hear a poem she wrote about it, when she was only fourteen years old.[20] It will help you, too, to think the same thoughts.

A little kingdom I possess,
        Where thoughts and feelings dwell,
And very hard I find the task
        Of governing it well;
For passion tempts and troubles me,
        A wayward will misleads,
And selfishness its shadow casts
        On all my words and deeds.

How can I learn to rule myself,
        To be the child I should,
Honest and brave, nor ever tire
        Of trying to be good?
How can I keep a sunny soul
        To shine along life's way?
How can I tune my little heart
        To sweetly sing all day?

Dear Father, help me with the love
        That casteth out my fear,
Teach me to lean on Thee, and feel
        That Thou art very near,
That no temptation is unseen,
        No childish grief too small,
Since Thou, with patience infinite,
        Doth soothe and comfort all.

I do not ask for any crown
        But that which all may win,
Nor seek to conquer any world,
        Except the one within.
Be Thou my Guide until I find,

Led by a tender hand,
Thy happy kingdom in*myself*,
And dare to take command.

PICCOLA[21]

Poor, sweet Piccola! Did you hear
What happened to Piccola, children dear?
'Tis seldom Fortune such favour grants
As fell to this little maid of France.

'Twas Christmas-time, and her parents poor
Could hardly drive the wolf from the door,
Striving with poverty's patient pain
Only to live till summer again.

No gifts for Piccola! Sad were they
When dawned the morning of Christmas-day;
Their little darling no joy might stir,
St Nicholas nothing would bring to her!

But Piccola never doubted at all
That something beautiful must befall
Every child upon Christmas-day,
And so she slept till the dawn was gray.

And full of faith, when at last she woke,
She stole to her shoe as the morning broke;
Such sounds of gladness filled all the air,
Twas plain St Nicholas had been there!

In rushed Piccola sweet, half wild:
Never was seen such a joyful child.

"See what the good saint brought!" she cried,
And mother and father must peep inside.

Now such a story who ever heard?
There was a little shivering bird!
A sparrow, that in at the window flew,
Had crept into Piccola's tiny shoe!

"How good poor Piccola must have been!"
She cried, as happy as any queen,
While the starving sparrow she fed and warmed,
And danced with rapture, she was so charmed.

Children, this story I tell to you,
Of Piccola sweet and her bird, is true.
In the far-off land of France, they say,
Still do they live to this very day.

THE LITTLE FIR TREE

When I was a very little girl some one, probably my mother, read to me Hans Christian Andersen's story of the Little Fir Tree. It happened that I did not read it for myself or hear it again during my childhood. One Christmas Day, when I was grown up, I found myself at a loss for the "one more" story called for by some little children with whom I was spending the holiday. In the mental search for buried treasure which ensued, I came upon one or two word-impressions of the experiences of the Little Fir Tree, and forthwith wove them into what I supposed to be something of a reproduction of the original. The latter part of the story had wholly faded from my memory, so that I "made up" to suit the tastes of my audience. Afterward I told the story to a good many children, at one time or another, and it gradually took the shape it has here. It was not until several years later that, in rereading Andersen for other purposes, I came upon the real story of the Little Fir Tree, and read it for myself. Then indeed I was amused, and somewhat distressed, to find how far I had wandered from the text.

I give this explanation that the reader may know I do not presume to offer the little tale which follows as an "adaptation" of Andersen's famous story. I offer it plainly as a story which children have liked, and which grew out of my early memories of Andersen's *The Little Fir Tree.*

Once there was a Little Fir Tree, slim and pointed, and shiny, which stood in the great forest in the midst of some big fir trees, broad, and tall, and shadowy green. The Little Fir Tree was very unhappy because he was not big like the others. When the birds came flying into the woods and lit on the branches of the big trees and built their nests there, he used to call up to them,—

"Come down, come down, rest in my branches!" But they always said,—

"Oh, no, no; you are too little!"

When the splendid wind came blowing and singing through the forest, it bent and rocked and swung the tops of the big trees, and murmured to them.

Then the Little Fir Tree looked up, and called,—

"Oh, please, dear wind, come down and play with me!" But he always said,—

"Oh, no; you are too little, you are too little!"

In the winter the white snow fell softly, softly, and covered the great trees all over with wonderful caps and coats of white. The Little Fir Tree, close down in the cover of the others, would call up,—

"Oh, please, dear snow, give me a cap, too! I want to play, too!" But the snow always said,—

"Oh no, no, no; you are too little, you are too little!"

The worst of all was when men came into the wood, with sledges and teams of horses. They came to cut the big trees down and carry them away. Whenever one had been cut down and carried away the others talked about it, and nodded their heads, and the Little Fir Tree listened, and heard them say that when you were carried away so, you might become the mast of a mighty ship, and go far away over the ocean, and see many wonderful things; or you might be part of a fine house in a great city, and see much of life. The Little Fir Tree wanted greatly to see life, but he was always too little; the men passed him by.

But by and by, one cold winter's morning, men came with a sledge and horses, and after they had cut here and there they came to the circle of trees round the Little Fir Tree, and looked all about.

"There are none little enough," they said.

Oh! how the Little Fir Tree pricked up his needles!

"Here is one," said one of the men, "it is just little enough." And he touched the Little Fir Tree.

The Little Fir Tree was happy as a bird, because he knew they were about to cut him down. And when he was being carried away on the sledge he lay wondering, *so* contentedly, whether he should be the mast of a ship or part of a fine city house. But when they came to the town he was taken out and set upright in a tub and placed on the edge of a path in a row of other fir trees, all small, but none so little as he. And then the Little Fir Tree began to see life.

People kept coming to look at the trees and to take them away. But always when they saw the Little Fir Tree they shook their heads and said,—

"It is too little, too little."

Until, finally, two children came along, hand in hand, looking carefully at all the small trees. When they saw the Little Fir Tree they cried out,—

"We'll take this one; it is just little enough!"

They took him out of his tub and carried him away, between them. And the happy Little Fir Tree spent all his time wondering what it could be that he was just little enough for; he knew it could hardly be a mast or a house, since he was going away with children.

He kept wondering, while they took him in through some big doors, and set him up in another tub, on the table, in a bare little room. Very soon they went away, and came back again with a big basket, which they carried between them. Then some pretty ladies, with white caps on their heads and white aprons over their blue dresses, came bringing little parcels. The children took things out of the basket and began to play with the Little Fir Tree, just as he had often begged the wind and the snow and the birds to do. He felt their soft little touches on his head and his twigs and his branches. When he looked down at himself, as far as he could look, he saw that he was all hung with gold and silver chains! There were strings of white fluffy stuff drooping around him; his twigs held little gold nuts and pink, rosy balls and silver stars; he had pretty little pink and white candles in his arms; but last, and most wonderful of all, the children hung a beautiful white, floating doll-angel over his head! The Little Fir Tree could not breathe, for joy and wonder. What was it that he was, now? Why was this glory for him?

After a time every one went away and left him. It grew dusk, and the Little Fir Tree began to hear strange sounds through the closed doors. Sometimes he heard a child crying. He was beginning to be lonely. It grew more and more shadowy.

All at once, the doors opened and the two children came in. Two of the pretty ladies were with them. They came up to the Little Fir Tree and quickly lighted all the little pink and white candles. Then the two pretty ladies took hold of the table with the Little Fir Tree on it and pushed it, very smoothly and quickly, out of the doors, across a hall, and in at another door.

The Little Fir Tree had a sudden sight of a long room with many little white beds in it, of children propped up on pillows in the beds, and of other children in great wheeled chairs, and others hobbling about or sitting in little chairs. He wondered why all the little children looked so white and tired; he did not know that he was in a hospital. But before he could wonder any more his breath was quite taken away by the shout those little white children gave.

"Oh! oh! m-m! m-m!" they cried.

"How pretty! How beautiful! Oh, isn't it lovely!"

He knew they must mean him, for all their shining eyes were looking straight at him. He stood as straight as a mast, and quivered in every needle, for joy. Presently one little weak child-voice called out,—

"It's the nicest Christmas tree I ever saw!"

And then, at last, the Little Fir Tree knew what he was; he was a Christmas tree! And from his shiny head to his feet he was glad, through and through, because he was just little enough to be the nicest kind of tree in the world!

HOW MOSES WAS SAVED

Thousands of years ago, many years before David lived, there was a very wise and good man of his people who was a friend and adviser of the king of Egypt. And for love of this friend, the king of Egypt had let numbers of the Israelites settle in his land. But after the king and his Israelitish friend were dead, there was a new king, who hated the Israelites. When he saw how strong they were, and how many there were of them, he began to be afraid that some day they might number more than the Egyptians, and might take his land from him.

Then he and his rulers did a wicked thing. They made the Israelites slaves. And they gave them terrible tasks to do, without proper rest, or food, or clothes. For they hoped that the hardship would kill off the Israelites. They thought the old men would die and the young men be so ill and weary that they could not bring up families, and so the race would dwindle away.

But in spite of the work and suffering, the Israelites remained strong, and more and more boys grew up, to make the king afraid.

Then he did the most wicked thing of all. He ordered his soldiers to kill every boy baby that should be born in an Israelitish family; he did not care about the girls, because they could not grow up to fight.

Very soon after this wicked order, a boy baby was born in a certain Israelitish family. When his mother first looked at him her heart was nearly broken, for he was even more beautiful than most babies are,—so strong and fair and sweet. But he was a boy! How could she save him from death?

Somehow, she contrived to keep him hidden for three whole months. But at the end of that time, she saw that it would not be possible to keep him safe any longer. She had been thinking all this time about what she should do, and now she carried out her plan.

First, she took a basket made of bulrushes and daubed it all over with pitch, so that it was water-tight, and then she laid the baby in it; then she carried it to the edge of the river and laid it in the flags by the river's brink. It did not show at all, unless one were quite near it. Then she kissed her little son and left him there. But his sister stood far off, not seeming to watch, but really watching carefully to see what would happen to the baby.

Soon there was the sound of talk and laughter, and a train of beautiful women came down to the water's edge. It was the king's daughter, come down to bathe in the river, with her maidens. The maidens walked along by the river side.

As the king's daughter came near to the water, she saw the strange little basket lying in the flags, and she sent her maid to bring it to her. And when she had opened it, she saw the child; the poor baby was crying. When she saw him, so helpless and so beautiful, crying for his mother, the king's daughter pitied him and loved him. She knew the cruel order of her father, and she said at once, "This is one of the Hebrews' children."

At that moment the baby's sister came to the princess and said, "Shall I go and find thee a nurse from the Hebrew women, so that she may nurse the child for thee?" Not a word did she say about whose child it was, but perhaps the princess guessed; I don't know. At all events, she told the little girl to go.

So the maiden went, and brought her mother!

Then the king's daughter said to the baby's mother, "Take this child away and nurse it for me, and I will give thee wages."

Was not that a strange thing? And can you think how happy the baby's mother was? For now the baby would be known only as the princess's adopted child, and would be safe.

And it was so. The mother kept him until he was old enough to be taken to the princess's palace. Then he was brought and given to the king's daughter, and he became her son. And she named him Moses.

But the strangest part of the whole story is, that when Moses grew to be a man he became so strong and wise that it was he who at last saved his people from the king and rescued them from the Egyptians. The one child saved by the king's own daughter was the very one the king would most have wanted to kill, if he had known.

THE TEN FAIRIES[22]

Once upon a time there was a dear little girl, whose name was Elsa. Elsa's father and mother worked very hard and became rich. But they loved Elsa so much that they did not like her to do any work; very foolishly, they let her play all the time. So when Elsa grew up, she did not know how to do anything; she could not make bread, she could not sweep a room, she could not sew a seam; she could only laugh and sing. But she was so sweet and merry that everybody loved her. And by and by, she married one of the people who loved her, and had a house of her own to take care of.

Then, then, my dears, came hard times for Elsa! There were so many things to be done in the house, and she did not know how to do any of them! And because she had never worked at all it made her very tired even to try; she was tired before the morning was over, every day. The maid would come and say, "How shall I do this?" or "How shall I do that?" and Elsa would have to say, "I don't know." Then the maid would pretend that she did not know, either; and when she saw her mistress sitting about doing nothing, she, too, sat about, idle.

Elsa's husband had a hard time of it; he had only poor food to eat, and it was not ready at the right time, and the house looked all in a muddle. It made him sad, and that made Elsa sad, for she wanted to do everything just right.

At last, one day, Elsa's husband went away quite cross; he said to her, as he went out of the door, "It is no wonder that the house looks so, when you sit all day with your hands in your lap!"

Little Elsa cried bitterly when he was gone, for she did not want to make her husband unhappy and cross, and she wanted the house to look nice. "Oh, dear," she sobbed, "I wish I could do things right! I wish I could work! I wish—I wish I had ten good fairies to work for me! Then I could keep the house!"

As she said the words, a great grey man stood before her; he was wrapped in a strange grey cloak that covered him from head to foot; and he smiled at Elsa. "What is the matter, dear?" he said. "Why do you cry?"

"Oh, I am crying because I do not know how to keep the house," said Elsa. "I cannot make bread, I cannot sweep, I cannot sew a seam; when I was a little girl I never learned to work, and now I cannot do anything right. I wish I had ten good fairies to help me!"

"You shall have them, dear," said the grey man, and he shook his strange grey cloak. Pouf! Out hopped ten tiny fairies, no bigger than that!

"These shall be your servants, Elsa," said the grey man; "they are faithful and clever, and they will do everything you want them to, just right. But the neighbours might stare and ask questions if they saw these little chaps running about your house, so I will hide them away for you. Give me your little useless hands."

Wondering, Elsa stretched out her pretty, little, white hands.

"Now stretch out your little useless fingers, dear!"

Elsa stretched out her pretty pink fingers.

The grey man touched each one of the ten little fingers, and as he touched them he said their names: "Little Thumb; Forefinger; Thimble-finger; Ring-finger; Little Finger; Little Thumb; Forefinger; Thimble-finger; Ring-finger; Little Finger!" And as he named the fingers, one after another, the tiny fairies bowed their tiny heads; there was a fairy for every name.

"Hop! hide yourselves away!" said the grey man.

Hop, hop! The fairies sprang to Elsa's knee, then to the palms of her hands, and then—whisk! they were all hidden away in her little pink fingers, a fairy in every finger! And the grey man was gone.

Elsa sat and looked with wonder at her little white hands and the ten useless fingers. But suddenly the little fingers began to stir. The tiny fairies who were hidden away there were not used to remaining still, and they were getting restless. They stirred so that Elsa jumped up and ran to the cooking table, and took hold of the bread board. No sooner had she touched the bread board than the little fairies began to work: they measured the flour, mixed the bread, kneaded the loaves, and set them to rise, quicker than you could wink; and when the bread was done, it was as nice as you could wish. Then the little fairy-fingers seized the broom, and in a twinkling they were making the house clean. And so it went, all day. Elsa flew about from one thing to another, and the ten fairies did the work, just right.

When the maid saw her mistress working, she began to work, too; and when she saw how beautifully everything was done, she was ashamed to do anything badly herself. In a little while the housework was going smoothly, and Elsa could laugh and sing again.

There was no more crossness in that house. Elsa's husband grew so proud of her that he went about saying to everybody, "My grandmother was a fine housekeeper, and my mother was a fine housekeeper, but neither of them could hold a candle to my wife. She has only one maid, but, to see the work done, you would think she had as many servants as she has fingers on her hands!"

When Elsa heard that, she used to laugh, but she never, never told.

THE ELVES AND THE SHOEMAKER

Once upon a time there was an honest shoemaker, who was very poor. He worked as hard as he could, and still he could not earn enough to keep himself and his wife. At last there came a day when he had nothing left but one piece of leather, big enough to make one pair of shoes. He cut out the shoes, ready to stitch, and left them on the bench; then he said his prayers and went to bed, trusting that he could finish the shoes on the next day and sell them.

Bright and early the next morning, he rose and went to his work bench. There lay a pair of shoes, beautifully made, and the leather was gone! There was no sign of anyone having been there. The shoemaker and his wife did not know what to make of it. But the first customer who came was so pleased with the beautiful shoes that he bought them, and paid so much that the shoemaker was able to buy leather enough for two pairs.

Happily, he cut them out, and then, as it was late, he left the pieces on the bench, ready to sew in the morning. But when morning came, two pairs of shoes lay on the bench, most beautifully made, and no sign of anyone who had been there. The shoemaker and his wife were quite at a loss.

That day a customer came and bought both pairs, and paid so much for them that the shoemaker bought leather for four pairs, with the money.

Once more he cut out the shoes and left them on the bench. And in the morning all four pairs were made.

It went on like this until the shoemaker and his wife were prosperous people. But they could not be satisfied to have so much done for them and not know to whom they should be grateful. So one night, after the shoemaker had left the pieces of leather on the bench, he and his wife hid themselves behind a curtain, and left a light in the room.

Just as the clock struck twelve the door opened softly, and two tiny elves came dancing into the room, hopped on to the bench, and began to put the pieces together. They were quite naked, but they had wee little scissors and hammers and thread. Tap! tap! went the little hammers; stitch, stitch, went the thread, and the little elves were hard at work. No one ever worked so fast as they. In almost no time all the shoes were stitched and finished. Then the tiny elves took hold of each other's hands and danced round the shoes on the bench, till the shoemaker and his wife had hard work not to laugh aloud. But as the clock struck two, the little creatures whisked away out of the window, and left the room all as it was before.

The shoemaker and his wife looked at each other, and said, "How can we thank the little elves who have made us happy and prosperous?"

"I should like to make them some pretty clothes," said the wife, "they are quite naked."

"I will make the shoes if you will make the coats," said her husband.

That very day they commenced their task. The wife cut out two tiny, tiny coats of green, two weeny, weeny waistcoats of yellow, two little pairs of trousers, of white, two bits of caps, bright red (for every one knows the elves love bright colours), and her husband made two little pairs of shoes with long, pointed toes. They made the wee clothes as dainty as could be, with nice little stitches and pretty buttons; and by Christmas time, they were finished.

On Christmas eve, the shoemaker cleaned his bench, and on it, instead of leather, he laid the two sets of gay little fairy-clothes. Then he and his wife hid away as before, to watch.

Promptly at midnight, the little naked elves came in. They hopped upon the bench; but when they saw the little clothes there, they laughed and danced for joy. Each one caught up his little coat and things and began to put them on. Then they looked at each other and made all kinds of funny motions in their delight. At last they began to dance, and when the clock struck two, they danced quite away, out of the window.

They never came back any more, but from that day they gave the shoemaker and his wife good luck, so that they never needed any more help.

WHO KILLED THE OTTER'S BABIES?[23]

Once the Otter came to the Mouse-deer and said, "Friend Mouse-deer, will you please take care of my babies while I go to the river, to catch fish?"

"Certainly," said the Mouse-deer, "go along."

But when the Otter came back from the river, with a string of fish, he found his babies crushed flat.

"What does this mean, Friend Mouse-deer?" he said. "Who killed my children while you were taking care of them?"

"I am very sorry," said the Mouse-deer, "but you know I am Chief Dancer of the War-dance, and the Woodpecker came and sounded the war-gong, so I danced. I forgot your children, and trod on them."

"I shall go to King Solomon," said the Otter, "and you shall be punished."

Soon the Mouse-deer was called before King Solomon.

"Did you kill the Otter's babies?" said the king.

"Yes, your Majesty," said the Mouse-deer, "but I did not mean to."

"How did it happen?" said the king.

"Your Majesty knows," said the Mouse-deer, "that I am Chief Dancer of the War-dance. The Woodpecker came and sounded the war-gong, and I had to dance; and as I danced I trod on the Otter's children."

"Send for the Woodpecker," said King Solomon. When the Woodpecker came, he said to him, "Was it you who sounded the war-gong?"

"Yes, your Majesty," said the Woodpecker, "but I had to."

"Why?" said the king.

"Your Majesty knows," said the Woodpecker, "that I am Chief Beater of the War-gong, and I sounded the gong because I saw the Great Lizard wearing his sword."

"Send for the Great Lizard," said King Solomon. When the Great Lizard came, he asked him, "Was it you who were wearing your sword?"

"Yes, your Majesty," said the Great Lizard; "but I had to."

"Why?" said the king.

"Your Majesty knows," said the Great Lizard, "that I am Chief Protector of the Sword. I wore my sword because the Tortoise came wearing his coat of mail."

So the Tortoise was sent for.

"Why did you wear your coat of mail?" said the king.

"I put it on, your Majesty," said the Tortoise, "because I saw the King-crab trailing his three-edged pike."

Then the King-crab was sent for.

"Why were you trailing your three-edged pike?" said King Solomon.

"Because, your Majesty," said the King-crab, "I saw that the Crayfish had shouldered his lance."

Immediately the Crayfish was sent for.

"Why did you shoulder your lance?" said the king.

"Because, your Majesty," said the Crayfish, "I saw the Otter coming down to the river to kill my children."

"Oh," said King Solomon, "if that is the case, the Otter killed the Otter's children. And the Mouse-deer cannot be blamed, by the law of the land!"

EARLY[24]

I like to lie and wait to see
    My mother braid her hair.
It is as long as it can be,
    And yet she doesn't care.
I love my mother's hair.

And then the way her fingers go;
    They look so quick and white,—
In and out, and to and fro,
    And braiding in the light,
And it is always right.

So then she winds it, shiny brown,
Around her head into a crown,
    Just like the day before.
And then she looks and pats it down,
    And looks a minute more;
While I stay here all still and cool.
Oh, isn't morning beautiful?

THE BRAHMIN, THE TIGER, AND THE JACKAL

Do you know what a Brahmin is? A Brahmin is a very good and gentle kind of man who lives in India, and who treats all the beasts as if they were his brothers. There is a great deal more to know about Brahmins, but that is enough for the story.

One day a Brahmin was walking along a country road when he came upon a Tiger, shut up in a strong iron cage. The villagers had caught him and shut him up there for his wickedness.

"Oh, Brother Brahmin, Brother Brahmin," said the Tiger, "please let me out, to get a little drink! I am so thirsty, and there is no water here."

"But Brother Tiger," said the Brahmin, "you know if I should let you out, you would spring on me and eat me up."

"Never, Brother Brahmin!" said the Tiger. "Never in the world would I do such an ungrateful thing! Just let me out a little minute, to get a little, little drink of water, Brother Brahmin!"

So the Brahmin unlocked the door and let the Tiger out. The moment he was out he sprang on the Brahmin, and was about to eat him up.

"But, Brother Tiger," said the Brahmin, "you promised you would not. It is not fair or just that you should eat me, when I set you free."

"It is perfectly right and just," said the Tiger, "and I shall eat you up."

However, the Brahmin argued so hard that at last the Tiger agreed to wait and ask the first five whom they should meet, whether it was fair for him to eat the Brahmin, and to abide by their decision.

The first thing they came to, to ask, was an old Banyan Tree, by the wayside. (A banyan tree is a kind of fruit tree.)

"Brother Banyan," said the Brahmin, eagerly, "does it seem to you right or just that this Tiger should eat me, when I set him free from his cage?"

The Banyan Tree looked down at them and spoke in a tired voice.

"In the summer," he said, "when the sun is hot, men come and sit in the cool of my shade and refresh themselves with the fruit of my branches. But when evening falls, and they are rested, they break my twigs and scatter my leaves, and stone my boughs for more fruit. Men are an ungrateful race. Let the Tiger eat the Brahmin."

The Tiger sprang to eat the Brahmin, but the Brahmin said,—

"Wait, wait; we have asked only one. We have still four to ask."

Presently they came to a place where an old Bullock was lying by the road. The Brahmin went up to him and said,—

"Brother Bullock, oh, Brother Bullock, does it seem to you a fair thing that this Tiger should eat me up, after I have just freed him from a cage?"

The Bullock looked up, and answered in a deep, grumbling voice,—

"When I was young and strong my master used me hard, and I served him well. I carried heavy loads and carried them far. Now that I am old and weak and cannot work, he leaves me without food or water, to die by the wayside. Men are a thankless lot. Let the Tiger eat the Brahmin."

The Tiger sprang, but the Brahmin spoke very quickly,—

"Oh, but this is only the second, Brother Tiger; you promised to ask five."

The Tiger grumbled a good deal, but at last he went on again with the Brahmin. And after a time they saw an Eagle, high overhead. The Brahmin called up to him imploringly,—

"Oh, Brother Eagle, Brother Eagle! Tell us if it seems to you fair that this Tiger should eat me up, when I have just saved him from a frightful cage?"

The Eagle soared slowly overhead a moment, then he came lower, and spoke in a thin, clear voice.

"I live high in the air," he said, "and I do no man any harm. Yet as often as they find my eyrie, men stone my young and rob my nest and shoot at me with arrows. Men are a cruel breed. Let the Tiger eat the Brahmin!"

The Tiger sprang upon the Brahmin, to eat him up; and this time the Brahmin had very hard work to persuade him to wait. At last he did persuade him, however, and they walked on together. And in a little while they saw an old Alligator, lying half buried in mud and slime, at the river's edge.

"Brother Alligator, oh, Brother Alligator!" said the Brahmin, "does it seem at all right or fair to you that this Tiger should eat me up, when I have just now let him out of a cage?"

The old Alligator turned in the mud, and grunted, and snorted; then he said,—

"I lie here in the mud all day, as harmless as a pigeon; I hunt no man, yet every time a man sees me, he throws stones at me, and pokes me with sharp sticks, and jeers at me. Men are a worthless lot. Let the Tiger eat the Brahmin!"

At this the Tiger was going to eat the Brahmin at once. The poor Brahmin had to remind him, again and again, that they had asked only four.

"Wait till we've asked one more! Wait until we see a fifth!" he begged.

Finally, the Tiger walked on with him.

After a time, they met the little Jackal, coming gaily down the road toward them.

"Oh, Brother Jackal, dear Brother Jackal," said the Brahmin, "give us your opinion! Do you think it right or fair that this Tiger should eat me, when I set him free from a terrible cage?"

"Beg pardon?" said the little Jackal.

"I said," said the Brahmin, raising his voice, "do you think it is fair that the Tiger should eat me, when I set him free from his cage?"

"Cage?" said the little Jackal, vacantly.

"Yes, yes, his cage," said the Brahmin. "We want your opinion. Do you think——"

"Oh," said the little Jackal, "you want my opinion? Then may I beg you to speak a little more loudly, and make the matter quite clear? I am a little slow of understanding. Now what was it?"

"Do you think," said the Brahmin, "it is right for this Tiger to eat me, when I set him free from his cage?"

"What cage?" said the little Jackal.

"Why, the cage he was in," said the Brahmin. "You see——"

"But I don't altogether understand," said the little Jackal. "You 'set him free,' you say?"

"Yes, yes, yes!" said the Brahmin. "It was this way: I was walking along, and I saw the Tiger——"

"Oh, dear, dear!" interrupted the little Jackal; "I never can see through it, if you go on like that, with a long story. If you really want my opinion you must make the matter clear. What sort of cage was it?"

"Why, a big, ordinary cage, an iron cage," said the Brahmin.

"That gives me no idea at all," said the little Jackal. "See here, my friends, if we are to get on with this matter you'd best show me the spot. Then I can understand in a jiffy. Show me the cage."

So the Brahmin, the Tiger, and the little Jackal walked back together to the spot where the cage was.

"Now, let us understand the situation," said the little Jackal. "Friend Brahmin, where were you?"

"I stood just here by the roadside," said the Brahmin.

"Tiger, and where were you?" said the little Jackal.

"Why, in the cage, of course," roared the Tiger.

"Oh, I beg your pardon, Father Tiger," said the little Jackal, "I really am *so* stupid; I cannot *quite* understand what happened. If you will have a little patience,—*how* were you in the cage? What position were you in?"

"I stood here," said the Tiger, leaping into the cage, "with my head over my shoulder, so."

"Oh, thank you, thank you," said the little Jackal, "that makes it *much* clearer; but I still don't *quite* understand—forgive my slow mind—why did you not come out, by yourself?"

"Can't you see that the door shut me in?" said the Tiger.

"Oh, I do beg your pardon," said the little Jackal. "I know I am very slow; I can never understand things well unless I see just how they were; if you could show me now exactly how that door works I am sure I could understand. How does it shut?"

"It shuts like this," said the Brahmin, pushing it to.

"Yes; but I don't see any lock," said the little Jackal, "does it lock on the outside?"

"It locks like this," said the Brahmin. And he shut and bolted the door!

"Oh, does it, indeed?" said the little Jackal. "Does it, *indeed*! Well, Brother Brahmin, now that it is locked, I should advise you to let it stay locked! As for you, my friend," he said to the Tiger, "I think you will wait a good while before you'll find anyone to let you out again!" Then he made a very low bow to the Brahmin.

"Good-bye, Brother," he said. "Your way lies that way, and mine lies this; good-bye!"

THE LITTLE JACKAL AND THE CAMEL

All these stories about the little Jackal that I have told you, show how clever the little Jackal was. But you know—if you don't, you will when you are grown up—that no matter how clever you are, sooner or later you surely meet some one who is more clever. It is always so in life. And it was so with the little Jackal. This is what happened.

The little Jackal was, as you know, exceedingly fond of shell-fish, especially of river crabs. Now there came a time when he had eaten all the crabs to be found on his own side of the river. He knew there must be plenty on the other side, if he could only get to them, but he could not swim.

One day he thought of a plan. He went to his friend the Camel, and said, —

"Friend Camel, I know a spot where the sugar-cane grows thick; I'll show you the way, if you will take me there."

"Indeed I will," said the Camel, who was very fond of sugar-cane. "Where is it?"

"It is on the other side of the river," said the little Jackal; "but we can manage it nicely, if you will take me on your back and swim over."

The Camel was perfectly willing, so the little Jackal jumped on his back, and the Camel swam across the river, carrying him. When they were safely over, the little Jackal jumped down and showed the Camel the sugar-cane field; then he ran swiftly along the river bank, to hunt for crabs; the Camel began to eat sugar-cane. He ate happily, and noticed nothing around him.

Now, you know, a Camel is very big, and a Jackal is very little. Consequently, the little Jackal had eaten his fill by the time the Camel had barely taken a mouthful. The little Jackal had no mind to wait for his slow friend; he wanted to be off home again, about his business. So he ran round and round the sugar-cane field, and as he ran he sang and shouted, and made a great hullabaloo.

Of course, the villagers heard him at once.

"There is a Jackal in the sugar-cane," they said; "he will dig holes and destroy the roots; we must go down and drive him out." So they came down, with sticks and stones. When they got there, there was no Jackal to be seen; but they saw the great Camel, eating away at the juicy sugar-cane. They ran at him and beat him, and stoned him, and drove him away half dead.

When they had gone, leaving the poor Camel half killed, the little Jackal came dancing back from somewhere or other.

"I think it's time to go home, now," he said; "don't you?"

"Well, you *are* a pretty friend!" said the Camel. "The idea of your making such a noise, with your shouting and singing! You brought this upon me. What in the world made you do it? Why did you shout and sing?"

"Oh, I don't know *why*" said the little Jackal,—"I always sing after dinner!"

"So?" said the Camel. "Ah, very well, let us go home now."

He took the little Jackal kindly on his back and started into the water. When he began to swim he swam out to where the river was the very deepest. There he stopped, and said,—

"Oh, Jackal!"

"Yes," said the little Jackal.

"I have the strangest feeling," said the Camel,—"I feel as if I must roll over."

"'Roll over'!" cried the Jackal. "My goodness, don't do that! If you do that, you'll drown me! What in the world makes you want to do such a crazy thing? Why should you want to roll over?"

"Oh, I don't know *why*," said the Camel slowly, "but I always roll over after dinner!"

So he rolled over.

And the little Jackal was drowned, for his sins, but the Camel came safely home.

THE GULLS OF SALT LAKE

The story I am going to tell you is about something that really happened, many years ago.

A brave little company of pioneers from the Atlantic coast crossed the Mississippi River and journeyed across the plains of Central North America in big covered wagons with many horses, and finally succeeded in climbing to the top of the great Rockies and down again into a valley in the very midst of the mountains. It was a valley of brown, bare, desert soil, in a climate where almost no rain falls; but the snow on the mountain-tops sent down little streams of pure water, the winds were gentle, and lying like a blue jewel at the foot of the western hills was a marvellous lake of salt water,—an inland sea. So the pioneers settled there and built themselves huts and cabins for the first winter.

It had taken them many months to make the terrible journey; many had died of weariness and illness on the way; many died of hardship during the winter; and the provisions they had brought in their wagons were so nearly gone that, by spring, they were living partly on roots, dug from the ground. All their lives now depended on the crops of grain and vegetables which they could raise in the valley. They made the barren land fertile by spreading water from the little streams over it,—what we call "irrigating"; and they planted enough corn and grain and vegetables for all the people. Every one helped, and every one watched for the sprouting, with hopes, and prayers, and careful eyes.

In good time the seeds sprouted, and the dry, brown earth was covered with a carpet of tender, green, growing things. No farmer's garden could have looked better than the great garden of the desert valley. And from day to day the little shoots grew and flourished till they were all well above the ground.

Then a terrible thing happened. One day, the men who were watering the crops saw a great number of crickets swarming over the ground at the edge of the gardens nearest the mountains. They were hopping from the barren places into the young, green crops, and as they settled down they ate the tiny shoots and leaves to the ground. More came, and more, and ever more, and as they came they spread out till they covered a big corner of the grain field. And still more and more, till it was like an army of black, hopping, crawling crickets, streaming down the side of the mountain to kill the crops.

The men tried to kill the crickets by beating them down, but the numbers were so great that it was like beating at the sea. Then they ran and told the terrible news, and all the village came to help. They started fires; they dug trenches and filled them with water; they ran wildly about in the fields, killing what they could. But while they fought in one place new armies of crickets marched down the mountain-sides and attacked the fields in other places. And at last the people fell on their knees and wept and cried in despair, for they saw starvation and death in the fields.

A few knelt to pray. Others gathered round and joined them, weeping. More left their useless struggles and knelt beside their neighbours. At last nearly all the people were kneeling on the desolate fields praying for deliverance from the plague of crickets.

Suddenly, from far off in the air toward the great salt lake, there was the sound of flapping wings. It grew louder. Some of the people looked up, startled. They saw, like a white cloud rising from the lake, a flock of sea gulls flying toward them. Snow-white in the sun, with great wings beating and soaring, in hundreds and hundreds, they rose and circled and came on.

"The gulls! the gulls!" was the cry. "What does it mean?"

The gulls flew overhead, with a shrill chorus of whimpering cries, and then, in a marvellous white cloud of outspread wings and hovering breasts, they settled down over the cultivated ground.

"Oh! woe! woe!" cried the people. "The gulls are eating what the crickets have left! they will strip root and branch!"

But all at once, someone called out,—

"No, no! See! they are eating the crickets! They are eating only the crickets!"

It was true. The gulls devoured the crickets in dozens, in hundreds, in swarms. They ate until they were gorged, and then they flew heavily back to the lake, only to come again with new appetite. And when at last they finished, they had stripped the fields of the army of crickets; and the people were saved.

To this day, in the beautiful city of Salt Lake, which grew out of that pioneer village, the little children are taught to love the sea gulls. And when they learn drawing and weaving in the schools, their first design is often a picture of a cricket and a gull.

THE NIGHTINGALE[25]

A long, long time ago, as long ago as when there were fairies, there lived an emperor in China, who had a most beautiful palace, all made of crystal. Outside the palace was the loveliest garden in the whole world, and farther away was a forest where the trees were taller than any other trees in the world, and farther away, still, was a deep wood. And in this wood lived a little Nightingale. The Nightingale sang so beautifully that everybody who heard her remembered her song better than anything else that he heard or saw. People came from all over the world to see the crystal palace and the wonderful garden and the great forest; but when they went home and wrote books about these things they always wrote, "But the Nightingale is the best of all."

At last it happened that the Emperor came upon a book which said this, and he at once sent for his Chamberlain.

"Who is this Nightingale?" said the Emperor. "Why have I never heard him sing?"

The Chamberlain, who was a very important person, said, "There cannot be any such person; I have never heard his name."

"The book says there is a Nightingale," said the Emperor. "I command that the Nightingale be brought here to sing for me this evening."

The Chamberlain went out and asked all the great lords and ladies and pages where the Nightingale could be found, but not one of them had ever heard of him. So the Chamberlain went back to the Emperor and said, "There is no such person."

"The book says there is a Nightingale," said the Emperor; "if the Nightingale is not here to sing for me this evening I will have the court trampled upon, immediately after supper."

The Chamberlain did not want to be trampled upon, so he ran out and asked everybody in the palace about the Nightingale. At last, a little girl who worked in the kitchen to help the cook, said, "Oh, yes, I know the Nightingale very well. Every night, when I go to carry scraps from the kitchen to my mother, who lives in the wood beyond the forest, I hear the Nightingale sing."

The Chamberlain asked the maid to take him to the Nightingale's home, and many of the lords and ladies followed after. When they had gone a little way, they heard a cow moo.

"Ah!" said the lords and ladies, "that must be the Nightingale; what a large voice for so small a creature!"

"Oh, no," said the little girl, "that is just a cow, mooing."

A little farther on they heard some bullfrogs, in a swamp. "Surely that is the Nightingale," said the courtiers; "it really sounds like church-bells!"

"Oh, no," said the little girl, "those are bullfrogs, croaking."

At last they came to the wood where the Nightingale was. "Hush!" said the little girl, "she is going to sing." And, sure enough, the little Nightingale began to sing. She sang so beautifully that you have never in all your life heard anything like it.

"Dear, dear," said the courtiers, "that is very pleasant; does that little grey bird really make all that noise? She is so pale that I think she has lost her colour for fear of us."

The Chamberlain asked the little Nightingale to come and sing for the Emperor. The little Nightingale said she could sing better in her own greenwood, but she was so sweet and kind that she came with them.

That evening the palace was all trimmed with the most beautiful flowers you can imagine, and rows and rows of little silver bells, that tinkled when the wind blew in, and hundreds and hundreds and hundreds of wax candles, that shone like tiny stars. In the great hall there was a gold perch for the Nightingale, beside the Emperor's throne.

When all the people were there, the Emperor asked the Nightingale to sing. Then the little grey Nightingale filled her throat full, and sang. And, my dears, she sang so beautifully that the Emperor's eyes filled up with tears! And, you know, emperors do not cry at all easily. So he asked her to sing again, and this time she sang so marvellously that the tears came out of his eyes and ran down his cheeks. That was a great success. They asked the little Nightingale to sing, over and over again, and when they had listened enough the Emperor said that she should be made "Singer in Chief to the Court." She was to have a golden perch near the Emperor's bed, and a little golden cage, and was to be allowed to go out twice every day. But there were twelve servants appointed to wait on her, and those twelve servants went with her every time she went out, and each of the twelve had hold of the end of a silken string which was tied to the little Nightingale's leg! It was not so very much fun to go out that way!

For a long, long time the Nightingale sang every evening to the Emperor and his court, and they liked her so much that the ladies all tried to sing like her; they used to put water in their mouths and then make little sounds like this: *glu-glu-glug*. And when the courtiers met each other in the halls, one would say "Night," and the other would say "ingale," and that was supposed to be conversation.

At last, one day, there came a little package to the Emperor, on the outside of which was written, "The Nightingale." Inside was an artificial bird, something like a Nightingale, only it was made of gold, and silver, and rubies, and emeralds, and diamonds. When it was wound up it played a waltz tune, and as it played it moved its little tail up and down. Everybody in the court was filled with delight at the music of the new nightingale. They made it sing that same tune thirty-three times, and still they had not had enough. They would have made it sing the tune thirty-four times, but the Emperor said, "I should like to hear the real Nightingale sing, now."

But when they looked about for the real little Nightingale, they could not find her anywhere! She had taken the chance, while everybody was listening to the waltz tunes, to fly away through the window to her own greenwood.

"What a very ungrateful bird!" said the lords and ladies. "But it does not matter; the new nightingale is just as good."

So the artificial nightingale was given the real Nightingale's little gold perch, and every night the Emperor wound her up, and she sang waltz tunes to him. The people in the court liked her even better than the old Nightingale, because they could all whistle her tunes,—which you can't do with real nightingales.

About a year after the artificial nightingale came, the Emperor was listening to her waltz tune, when there was a *snap* and *whir-r-r* inside the bird, and the music stopped. The Emperor ran to his doctor, but he could not do anything. Then he ran to his clock-maker, but he could not do much. Nobody could do much. The best they could do was to patch the gold nightingale up so that it could sing once a year; even that was almost too much, and the tune was very shaky. Still, the Emperor kept the gold nightingale on the perch in his own room.

A long time went by, and then, at last, the Emperor grew very ill, and was about to die. When it was sure that he could not live much longer, the people chose a new emperor and waited for the old one to die. The poor Emperor lay, quite cold and pale, in his great big bed, with velvet curtains and tall candlesticks all about. He was quite alone, for all the courtiers had gone to congratulate the new emperor, and all the servants had gone to talk it over.

When the Emperor woke up, he felt a terrible weight on his chest. He opened his eyes, and there was Death, sitting on his heart. Death had put on the Emperor's gold crown, and he had the gold sceptre in one hand, and the silken banner in the other; and he looked at the Emperor with his great hollow eyes. The room was full of shadows, and the shadows were full of faces. Everywhere the Emperor looked, there were faces. Some were very, very ugly, and some were sweet and lovely; they were all the things the Emperor had done in his life, good and bad. And as he looked at them they began to whisper. They whispered, "*Do you remember this?*" "*Do you remember that?*" The Emperor remembered so much that he cried out loud, "Oh, bring the great drum! Make music, so that I may not hear these dreadful whispers!" But there was nobody there to bring the drum.

Then the Emperor cried, "You little gold nightingale, can you not sing something for me? I have given you gifts of gold and jewels, and kept you always by my side; will you not help me now?" But there was nobody to wind the little gold nightingale up, and of course it could not sing.

The Emperor's heart grew colder and colder where Death crouched upon it, and the dreadful whispers grew louder and louder, and the Emperor's life was almost gone. Suddenly, through the open window, there came a most lovely song. It was so sweet and so loud that the whispers died quite away. Presently the Emperor felt his heart grow warm, then he felt the blood flow through his limbs again; he listened to the song until the tears ran down his cheeks; he knew that it was the little real Nightingale who had flown away from him when the gold nightingale came.

Death was listening to the song, too; and when it was done and the Emperor begged for more, Death, too, said, "Please sing again, little Nightingale!"

"Will you give me the Emperor's gold crown for a song?" said the little Nightingale.

"Yes," said Death; and the little Nightingale bought the Emperor's crown for a song.

"Oh, sing again, little Nightingale," begged Death.

"Will you give me the Emperor's sceptre for another song?" said the little grey Nightingale.

"Yes," said Death; and the little Nightingale bought the Emperor's sceptre for another song.

Once more Death begged for a song, and this time the little Nightingale obtained the banner for her singing. Then she sang one more song, so sweet and so sad that it made Death think of his garden in the churchyard, where he always liked best to be. And he rose from the Emperor's heart and floated away through the window.

When Death was gone, the Emperor said to the little Nightingale, "Oh, dear little Nightingale, you have saved me from Death! Do not leave me again. Stay with me on this little gold perch, and sing to me always!"

"No, dear Emperor," said the little Nightingale, "I sing best when I am free; I cannot live in a palace. But every night when you are quite alone, I will come and sit in the window and sing to you, and tell you everything that goes on in your kingdom: I will tell you where the poor people are who ought to be helped, and where the wicked people are who ought to be punished. Only, dear Emperor, be sure that you never let anybody know that you have a little bird who tells you everything."

After the little Nightingale had flown away, the Emperor felt so well and strong that he dressed himself in his royal robes and took his gold sceptre in his hand. And when the courtiers came in to see if he were dead, there stood the Emperor with his sword in one hand and his sceptre in the other, and said, "Good-morning!"

MARGERY'S GARDEN[26]

There was once a little girl named Margery, who had always lived in the city. The flat where her mother and father lived was at the top of a big building, and you couldn't see a great deal from the windows, except chimney-pots on other people's roofs. Margery did not know much about trees and flowers, but she loved them dearly; whenever it was a fine Sunday she used to go with her mother and father to the park and look at the lovely flower-beds. They seemed always to be finished, though, and Margery was always wishing she could see them grow.

One spring, when Margery was nine, her father obtained a new situation and they removed to a little house with a nice big piece of ground a short distance outside the town where his new position was. Margery was delighted. And the very first thing she said, when her father told her about it, was, "Oh, may I have a garden? *May* I have a garden?"

Margery's mother was almost as eager for a garden as she was, and Margery's father said he expected to live on their vegetables all the rest of his life! So it was soon agreed that the garden should be the first thing attended to.

Behind the cottage were apple trees, a plum tree, and two or three pear trees; then came a stretch of rough grass, and then a stone wall, with a gate leading into the fields. It was on the grass plot that the garden was to be. A big piece was to be used for wheat and peas and beans, and a little piece at the end was to be given to Margery.

"What shall we have in it?" asked her mother.

"Flowers," said Margery, with shining eyes,—"blue, and white, and yellow, and pink,—every kind of flower!"

"Surely, flowers," said her mother, "and shall we not have a little salad garden in the middle?"

"What is a salad garden?" Margery asked.

"It is a garden where you have all the things that make nice salad," said her mother, laughing, for Margery was fond of salads; "you have lettuce, and endive, and mustard and cress, and parsley, and radishes, and beetroot, and young onions."

"Oh! how good it sounds!" said Margery. "I should love a salad garden."

That very evening, Margery's father took pencil and paper, and drew out a plan for her garden; first, they talked it all over, then he drew what they decided on; it looked like the diagram on the next page.

"The outside strip is for flowers," said Margery's father, "and next is a footpath, all the way round the beds; that is to let you get at the flowers to weed and to pick; there is a wider path through the middle, and the rest is for rows of salad vegetables."

"Papa, it is glorious!" said Margery.

Papa laughed. "I hope you will still think it glorious when the weeding time comes," he said, "for you know, you and mother have promised to take care of this garden, while I take care of the big one."

"I wouldn't *not* take care of it for anything!" said Margery. "I want to feel that it is my very own."

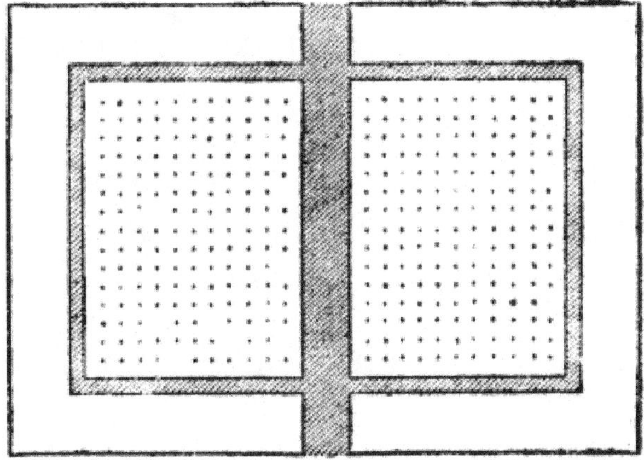

Her father kissed her, and said it was certainly her "very own."

Two evenings after that, when Margery was called in from her first ramble in the fields, she found the postman at the door.

"Something for you, Margery," said her mother, with the look she had when something nice was happening.

It was a box, quite a big box, with a label on it that said:—

Miss Margery Brown,
Primrose Cottage,
21 Narcissus Road,
Colchester.

From Seeds and Plants Company, Reading.

Margery could hardly wait to open it. It was filled with little packages, all with printed labels; and in the packages, of course, were seeds. It made Margery dance, just to read the names,—nasturtium, giant helianthus, canariensis, calendula, Canterbury bells: more names than I can tell you; and other packages, bigger, that said, "Sweet Peas," "French beans," "Carrots," "Wallflowers," and such things! Margery could almost smell the posies, she was so excited. Only, she had seen so little of flowers that she did not know what all the names meant. She did not know that a helianthus was a sunflower until her mother told her so, and she had never seen the dear, blue, bell-shaped flowers that always grow in old-fashioned gardens, and are called Canterbury bells. She thought the calendula must be a strange, grand flower, by its name; but her mother told her it was the gay, sturdy, everydayish little flower called a marigold. There was a great deal for a little city girl to be surprised about, and it did seem as if morning was a long way off!

"Did you think you could plant them in the morning?" asked her mother. "You know, dear, the ground has to be made ready first; it takes a little time, —it may be several days before you can plant."

That was another surprise. Margery had thought she could begin to sow the seed right off.

But this was what had happened. Early the next morning, a man came driving up to the cottage with two strong white horses; in his wagon was a plough. I suppose you have seen ploughs, but Margery never had, and she watched with great interest, while the man and her father took the plough from the cart and harnessed the horses to it. It was a great, three-cornered piece of sharp steel, with long handles coming up from it, so that a man could hold it in place. It looked like this:—

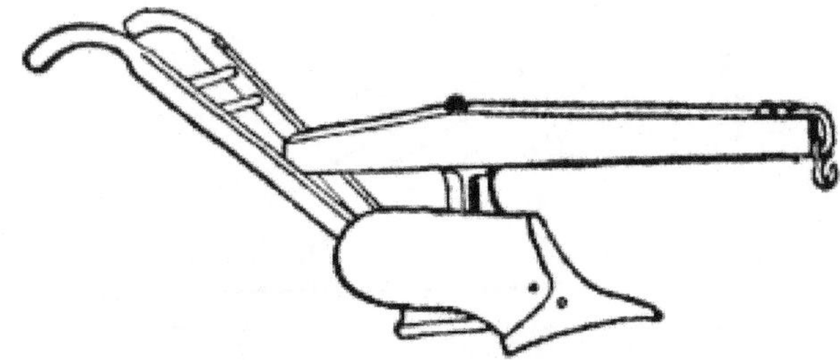

"I brought a two-horse plough because it's virgin soil," the man said. Margery wondered what in the world he meant; it had not been cultivated, of course, but what had that do with the kind of plough? "What does he mean, father?" she whispered, when she got a chance. "He means that this land has not been ploughed before; it will be hard to turn the soil, and one horse could not pull the plough," said her father.

It took the man two hours to plough the little strip of land. He drove the sharp end of the plough into the soil, and held it firmly so, while the horses drew it along in a straight line. Margery found it fascinating to watch the long line of dark earth and green grass come rolling up and turn over, as the knife passed it. She could see that it took real skill and strength to keep the line even, and to avoid the stones. Sometimes the plough struck a hidden stone, and then the man was jerked almost off his feet. But he only laughed, and said, "Tough piece of land; it will be a lot better next year."

When he had ploughed, the man went back to his cart and unloaded another farm implement. This one was like a three-cornered platform of wood, with a long, curved, strong rake under it. It was called a harrow, and it looked like the diagram on the next page.

The man harnessed the horses to it, and then he stood on the platform and drove all over the strip of land. It was fun to watch, but perhaps it was a little hard to do. The man's weight kept the harrow steady, and let the teeth of the rake scratch and cut the ground up, so that it did not stay in ridges.

"He scrambles the ground, father!" said Margery.

"It needs 'scrambling,'" laughed her father. "We are going to get more weeds than we want on this fresh soil, and the more the ground is broken, the fewer there will be."

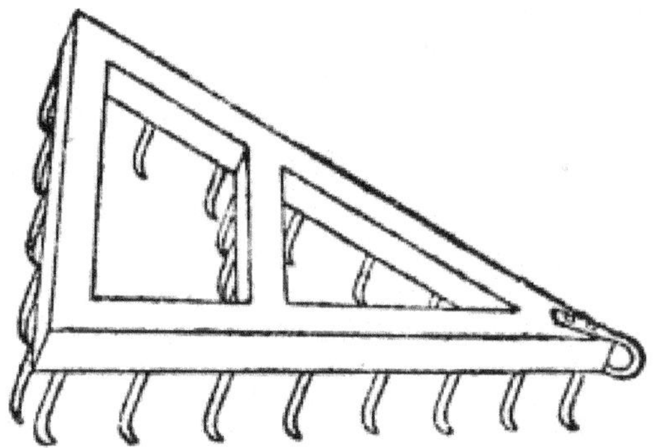

After the ploughing and harrowing, the man drove off, and Margery's father said that he himself would do the rest of the work in the late afternoons, when he came home from business; they could not afford too much help, he said, and he had learned to take care of a garden when he was a boy. So Margery did not see any more done until the next day.

But the next day there was hard work for Margery's father! Every bit of that ground had to be broken up still more with a spade, and then the clods which were full of grass-roots had to be taken on a fork and shaken, till the earth fell out; when the grass was thrown to one side. That would not have had to be done if the land had been ploughed in the autumn; the grass would have rotted in the ground, and would have made food for the plants. Now, Margery's father put the fertiliser on the top, and then raked it into the earth.

At last, it was time to make the place for the seeds. Margery and her mother helped. Father tied one end of a cord to a little stake, and drove the stake in the ground at one end of the garden. Then he took the cord to the other end of the garden and pulled it tight, tied it to another stake, and drove that down. That made a straight line. Then he hoed a trench, a few inches deep, the whole length of the cord, and scattered fertiliser in it. Pretty soon the whole garden was lined with little trenches.

"Now for the seed," said father.

Margery ran and brought the seed box. "May I help?" she asked.

"If you watch me sow one row, I think you can do the next," said her father.

So Margery watched. Her father took a handful of peas, and, stooping, walked slowly along the line, letting the seed trickle through his fingers. It was pretty to watch; it made Margery think of a photograph her teacher had, a photograph of a famous picture called "The Sower." Perhaps you have seen it.

Putting in the seed was not so easy to do as to watch; sometimes Margery dropped in too much, and sometimes not enough; but her father was patient with her, and soon she did better.

They planted peas, beans, spinach, carrots, and parsnips. And Margery's father made a row of holes, after that, for the tomato plants. He said those had to be transplanted; they could not be sown from seed.

When the seeds were in the trenches they had to be covered up, and Margery really helped at that. It is fun to do it. You stand beside the little trench and walk backward, and as you walk you hoe the loose earth back over the seeds; the same earth that was hoed up you pull back again. Then you rake very gently over the surface, with the back of a rake, to even it all off. Margery liked it, because now the garden began to look *like* a garden.

But best of all was the work next day, when her own little particular garden was begun. Father Brown loved Margery and Margery's mother so much that he wanted their garden to be perfect, and that meant a great deal more work. He knew very well that the old grass would begin to come through again on such soil, and that it would make terribly hard weeding. He was not going to have any such thing for his two "little girls," as he called them. So he gave that little garden particular attention. This is what he did.

After he had thrown out all the turf, he shovelled clean earth on to the garden,—as much as three solid inches of it; not a bit of grass was in that. Then it was ready for raking and fertilising, and for the lines. The little footpaths were marked out by Father Brown's feet; Margery and her mother laughed well at his actions, for it looked like some kind of dance. Mr Brown had seen gardeners do it when he was a little boy, and he did it very nicely: he walked along the sides of the square, with one foot turned a little out, and the other straight, taking such tiny steps that his feet touched each other all the time. This tramped out a path just wide enough for a person to walk.

The wider path was marked with lines and raked.

Margery thought, of course, all the flowers would be put in as the vegetables were; but she found that it was not so. For some, her father poked little holes with his finger; for some, he made very shallow trenches; and some very small seeds were scattered lightly over the top of the ground.

Margery and her mother had taken so much pains in thinking out the arrangement of the flowers, that perhaps you will like to hear just how they designed that garden. At the back were the sweet peas, which would grow tall, like a screen; on the two sides, for a kind of hedge, were yellow sunflowers; and along the front edge were the gay nasturtiums. Margery planned that, so that she could look into the garden from the front, but have it shut away from the vegetable patch by the tall flowers on the sides. The two front corners had canariensis in them. Canariensis is a pretty creeper with golden blossoms, very dainty and bright. And then, in little square patches all round the garden, were planted London pride, blue bachelor's buttons, yellow marigolds, tall larkspur, many-coloured asters, hollyhocks and stocks. All these lovely flowers used to grow in our grandmothers' gardens, and if you don't know what they look like, I hope you can find out next summer.

Between the flowers and the middle path went the seeds for that wonderful salad garden; all the things Mrs Brown had named to Margery were there. Margery had never seen anything more wonderful than the little round lettuce-seeds. They were so tiny that it did not seem possible that green lettuce leaves could come from them. But they surely would.

Mother and father and Margery were late to supper that evening. But they were all so happy that it did not matter. The last thing Margery thought of, as she went to sleep at night, was the dear, smooth little garden, with its funny footpath, and with the little sticks standing at the ends of the rows, labelled "lettuce," "beets," "helianthus," and so on.

"I have a garden! I have a garden!" was Margery's last thought as she went off to dreamland.

THE LITTLE COTYLEDONS

This is another story about Margery's garden.

The next morning after the garden was planted, Margery was up and out at six o'clock. She could not wait to look at her garden. To be sure, she knew that the seeds could not sprout in a single night, but she had a feeling that *something* might happen at any moment. The garden was just as smooth and brown as the night before, and no little seedlings were in sight.

But a very few mornings after that, when Margery went out, she saw a funny little crack opening up through the earth, the whole length of the patch. Quickly she knelt down on the footpath, to see. Yes! Tiny green leaves, a whole row of them, were pushing their way through the crust! Margery knew what she had put there: it was the radish-row; these must be radish leaves. She examined them very closely, so that she might know a radish next time. The little leaves, no bigger than half your little-finger nail, grew in twos,—two on each tiny stem; they were almost round.

Margery flew back to her mother, to say that the first seeds were up. And her mother, nearly as excited as Margery, came to look at the little crack.

Each day, after that, the row of radishes grew, till, in a week, it stood as high as your finger, green and sturdy. But about the third day, while Margery was stooping over the radishes, she saw something very, very small and green, peeping above ground, where the lettuce was planted. Could it be weeds? No, for on looking very closely she saw that the wee leaves faintly marked a regular row. They did not make a crack, like the radishes; they seemed too small and too far apart to push the earth up like that. Margery leaned down and looked with all her eyes at the baby plants. The tiny leaves grew two on a stem, and were almost round. The more she looked at them the more it seemed to Margery that they looked exactly as the radish looked when it first came up. "Do you suppose," Margery said to herself, "that lettuce and radish look alike while they are growing? They don't look alike when they are on the table!"

Day by day the lettuce grew, and soon the little round leaves were easier to examine; they certainly were very much like radish leaves.

Then, one morning, while she was searching for signs of other seeds, Margery discovered the beets. In irregular patches on the row, hints of green were coming. The next day and the next they grew, until the beet leaves were big enough to see.

Margery looked. Then she looked again. Then she wrinkled her forehead. "Can we have made a mistake?" she thought. "Do you suppose we can have planted *all* radishes?"

For those little beet leaves were almost round, and they grew two on a stem, precisely like the lettuce and the radish; except for the size, all three rows looked alike.

It was too much for Margery. She ran to the house and found her father. Her little face was so anxious that he thought something unpleasant had happened. "Papa," she said, all out of breath, "do you think we could have made a mistake about my garden? Do you think we could have put radishes in all the rows?"

Father laughed. "What makes you think such a thing?" he asked.

"Papa," said Margery, "the little leaves all look exactly alike! every plant has just two tiny leaves on it, and shaped the same; they are roundish, and grow out of the stem at the same place."

Papa's eyes began to twinkle. "Many of the dicotyledonous plants look alike at the beginning," he said, with a little drawl on the big word. That was to tease Margery, because she always wanted to know the big words she heard.

"What's 'dicotyledonous'?" said Margery, carefully.

"Wait till I come home to-night, dear," said her father, "and I'll tell you."

That evening Margery was waiting eagerly for him. When her father finished his supper they went together to the garden, and father examined the seedlings carefully. Then he pulled up a little radish plant and a tiny beet.

"These little leaves," he said, "are not the real leaves of the plant; they are only little pockets to hold food for the plant to live on till it gets strong enough to push up into the air. As soon as the real leaves come out and begin to draw food from the air, these little substitutes wither up and fall off. These two lie folded up in the little seed from the beginning, and are full of plant food. They don't have to be very special in shape, you see, because they don't stay on the plant after it is grown up."

"Then every plant looks like this at first?" said Margery.

"No, dear, not every one; plants are divided into two kinds: those which have two food leaves, like these plants, and those which have only one; these are called dicotyledonous, and the ones which have but one food leaf are monocotyledonous. Many of the dicotyledons look alike."

"I think that is interesting," said Margery.

"I always, supposed the plants were different from the minute they began to grow."

"Indeed, no," said father. "Even some of the trees look like this when they first come through; you would not think a birch tree could look like a vegetable or a flower, would you? But it does, at first; it looks so much like these things that in the great nurseries, where trees are raised for forests and parks, the workmen have to be very carefully trained, or else they would pull up the trees when they are weeding. They have to be taught the difference between a birch tree and a weed."

"How funny!" said Margery, dimpling.

"Yes, it sounds funny," said father; "but, you see, the birch tree is dicotyledonous, and so are many weeds, and the dicotyledons look so much alike at first."

"I am glad to know that, father," said Margery, soberly. "I believe I shall learn a good deal from living in the country; don't you think so?"

Margery's father took her in his arms. "I hope so, dear," he said; "the country is a good place for little girls."

And that was all that happened, that day.

THE TALKATIVE TORTOISE[27]

Once upon a time, a Tortoise lived in a pond with two Ducks, who were her very good friends. She enjoyed the company of the Ducks, because she could talk with them to her heart's content; the Tortoise liked to talk. She always had something to say, and she liked to hear herself say it.

After many years of this pleasant living, the pond became very low, in a dry season; and finally it dried up. The two Ducks saw that they could no longer live there, so they decided to fly to another region, where there was more water. They went to the Tortoise to bid her good-bye.

"Oh, don't leave me behind!" begged the Tortoise. "Take me with you; I must die if I am left here."

"But you cannot fly!" said the Ducks. "How can we take you with us?"

"Take me with you! take me with you!" said the Tortoise.

The Ducks felt so sorry for her that at last they thought of a way to take her. "We have thought of a way which will be possible," they said, "if only you can manage to keep still long enough. We will each take hold of one end of a stout stick, and do you take the middle in your mouth; then we will fly up in the air with you and carry you with us. But remember not to talk! If you open your mouth, you are lost."

The Tortoise said she would not say a word; she would not so much as move her mouth; and she was very grateful. So the Ducks brought a strong little stick and took hold of the ends, while the Tortoise bit firmly on the middle. Then the two Ducks rose slowly in the air and flew away with their burden.

When they were above the treetops, the Tortoise wanted to say, "How high we are!" But she remembered, and kept still. When they passed the church steeple she wanted to say, "What is that which shines?" But she remembered, and held her peace. Then they came over the village square, and the people looked up and saw them. "Look at the Ducks carrying a

Tortoise!" they shouted; and every one ran to look. The Tortoise wanted to say, "What business is it of yours?" But she didn't. Then she heard the people shout, "Isn't it strange! Look at it! Look!"

The Tortoise forgot everything except that she wanted to say, "Hush, you foolish people!" She opened her mouth,—and fell to the ground. And that was the end of the Tortoise.

It is a very good thing to be able to hold one's tongue!

ROBERT OF SICILY[28]

An old legend says that there was once a king named Robert of Sicily, who was brother to the Great Pope of Rome and to the Emperor of Allemaine. He was a very selfish king, and very proud; he cared more for his pleasures than for the needs of his people, and his heart was so filled with his own greatness that he had no thought for God.

One day, this proud king was sitting in his place at church, at vesper service; his courtiers were about him, in their bright garments, and he himself was dressed in his royal robes. The choir was chanting the Latin service, and as the beautiful voices swelled louder, the king noticed one particular verse which seemed to be repeated again and again. He turned to a learned clerk at his side and asked what those words meant, for he knew no Latin.

"They mean, 'He hath put down the mighty from their seats, and hath exalted them of low degree,'" answered the clerk.

"It is well the words are in Latin, then," said the king angrily, "for they are a lie. There is no power on earth or in heaven which can put me down from my seat!" and he sneered at the beautiful singing, as he leaned back in his place.

Presently the king fell asleep, while the service went on. He slept deeply and long. When he awoke the church was dark and still, and he was all alone. He, the king, had been left alone in the church, to awake in the dark! He was furious with rage and surprise, and, stumbling through the dim aisles, he reached the great doors and beat at them, madly, shouting for his servants.

The old sexton heard some one shouting and pounding in the church, and thought it was some drunken vagabond who had stolen in during the service. He came to the door with his keys and called out, "Who is there?"

"Open! open! It is I, the king!" came a hoarse, angry voice from within.

"It is a crazy man," thought the sexton; and he was frightened. He opened the doors carefully and stood back, peering into the darkness. Out past him rushed the figure of a man in tattered, scanty clothes, with unkempt hair and white, wild face. The sexton did not know that he had ever seen him before, but he looked long after him, wondering at his wildness and his haste.

In his fluttering rags, without hat or cloak, not knowing what strange thing had happened to him, King Robert rushed to his palace gates, pushed aside the startled servants, and hurried, blind with rage, up the wide stair and through the great corridors, toward the room where he could hear the sound of his courtiers' voices. Men and women servants tried to stop the ragged man, who had somehow got into the palace, but Robert did not even see them as he fled along. Straight to the open doors of the big banquet hall he made his way, and into the midst of the grand feast there.

The great hall was filled with lights and flowers; the tables were set with everything that is delicate and rich to eat; the courtiers, in their gay clothes, were laughing and talking; and at the head of the feast, on the king's own throne, sat a king. His face, his figure, his voice were exactly like Robert of Sicily; no human being could have told the difference; no one dreamed that he was not the king. He was dressed in the king's royal robes, he wore the royal crown, and on his hand was the king's own ring. Robert of Sicily, half naked, ragged, without a sign of his kingship on him, stood before the throne and stared with fury at this figure of himself.

The king on the throne looked at him. "Who art thou, and what dost thou here?" he asked. And though his voice was just like Robert's own, it had something in it sweet and deep, like the sound of bells.

"I am the king!" cried Robert of Sicily. "I am the king, and you are an impostor!"

The courtiers started from their seats, and drew their swords. They would have killed the crazy man who insulted their king; but he raised his hand and stopped them, and with his eyes looking into Robert's eyes he said, "Not the king; you shall be the king's jester! You shall wear the cap and bells, and make laughter for my court. You shall be the servant of the servants, and your companion shall, be the jester's ape."

With shouts of laughter, the courtiers drove Robert of Sicily from the banquet hall; the waiting-men, with laughter, too, pushed him into the soldiers' hall; and there the pages brought the jester's wretched ape, and put a fool's cap and bells on Robert's head. It was like a terrible dream; he could not believe it true, he could not understand what had happened to him. And when he woke next morning, he believed it was a dream, and that he was king again. But as he turned his head, he felt the coarse straw under his cheek instead of the soft pillow, and he saw that he was in the stable, with the shivering ape by his side. Robert of Sicily was a jester, and no one knew him for the king.

Three long years passed. Sicily was happy and all things went well under the king, who was not Robert. Robert was still the jester, and his heart grew harder and more bitter with every year. Many times, during the three years, the king, who had his face and voice, had called him to himself, when none else could hear, and had asked him the one question, "Who art thou?" And each time that he asked it his eyes looked into Robert's eyes, to find his heart. But each time Robert threw back his head and answered, proudly, "I am the king!" And the other king's eyes grew sad and stern.

At the end of three years, the Pope called the Emperor of Allemaine and the King of Sicily, his brothers, to a great meeting in his city of Rome. The King of Sicily went, with all his soldiers and courtiers and servants,—a great procession of horsemen and footmen. Never had there been seen a finer sight than the grand train, men in bright armour, riders in wonderful cloaks of velvet and silk, servants, carrying marvellous presents to the Pope. And at the very end rode Robert, the jester. His horse was poor and old, many-coloured, and the ape rode with him. Every one in the villages through which they passed ran after the jester, and pointed and laughed.

The Pope received his brothers and their trains in the square before Saint Peter's. With music and flags and flowers he made the King of Sicily welcome, and greeted him as his brother. In the midst of it, the jester broke through the crowd and threw himself before the Pope. "Look at me!" he cried; "I am your brother, Robert of Sicily! This man is an impostor, who has stolen my throne. I am Robert, the king!"

The Pope looked at the poor jester with pity, but the Emperor of Allemaine turned to the King of Sicily, and said, "Is it not rather dangerous, brother, to keep a madman as jester?" And again Robert was pushed back among the serving-men.

It was Holy Week, and the king and the emperor, with all their trains, went every day to the great services in the cathedral. Something wonderful and holy seemed to make these services more beautiful than ever before. All the people of Rome felt it: it was as if the presence of an angel were there. Men thought of God, and felt His blessing on them. But no one knew who it was that brought the beautiful feeling. And when Easter Day came, never had there been so lovely, so holy a day: in the great churches, filled with flowers, and sweet with incense, the kneeling people listened to the choirs singing, and it was like the voices of angels; their prayers were more earnest than ever before, their praise more glad; there was something heavenly in Rome.

Robert of Sicily went to the services with the rest, and sat in the humblest place with the servants. Over and over again he heard the sweet voices of the choirs chant the Latin words he had heard long ago: *He hath put down the mighty from their seat, and hath exalted them of low degree.* And at last, as he listened, his heart was softened. He, too, felt the strange blessed presence of a heavenly power. He thought of God, and of his own wickedness; he remembered how selfish he had been, and how little good he had done; he realised, that his power had not been from himself, at all. On Easter night, as he crept to his bed of straw, he wept, not because he was so wretched, but because he had not been a better king when power was his.

At last all the festivities were over, and the King of Sicily went home to his own land again, with his people. Robert the jester came home too.

On the day of their home-coming, there was a special service in the royal church, and even after the service was over for the people, the monks held prayers of thanksgiving and praise. The sound of their singing came softly in at the palace windows. In the great banquet room, the king sat, wearing his royal robes and his crown, while many subjects came to greet him. At last, he sent them all away, saying he wanted to be alone; but he commanded the jester to stay. And when they were alone together the king looked into Robert's eyes, as he had done before, and said, softly, "Who art thou?"

Robert of Sicily bowed his head. "Thou knowest best," he said, "I only know that I have sinned."

As he spoke, he heard the voices of the monks singing, *He hath put down the mighty from their seat,*—and his head sank lower. But suddenly the music seemed to change; a wonderful light shone all about. As Robert raised his eyes, he saw the face of the king smiling at him with a radiance like nothing on earth, and as he sank to his knees before the glory of that smile, a voice sounded with the music, like a melody throbbing on a single string,—

"I am an angel, and thou art the king!"

Then Robert of Sicily was alone. His royal robes were upon him once more; he wore his crown and his royal ring. He was king. And when the courtiers came back they found their king kneeling by his throne, absorbed in silent prayer.

THE JEALOUS COURTIERS[29]

I wonder if you have ever heard the anecdote about the artist of Düsseldorf and the jealous courtiers. This is it. It seems there was once a very famous artist who lived in the little town of Düsseldorf. He did such fine work that the Elector, Prince Johann Wilhelm, ordered a portrait statue of himself, on horseback, to be done in bronze. The artist was overjoyed at the commission, and worked early and late at the statue.

At last the work was done, and the artist had the great statue set up in the public square of Düsseldorf, ready for the opening view. The Elector came on the appointed day, and with him came his favourite courtiers from the castle. Then the statue was unveiled. It was very beautiful,—so beautiful that the prince exclaimed in surprise. He could not look enough, and presently he turned to the artist and shook hands with him, like an old friend. "Herr Grupello," he said, "you are a great artist, and this statue will make your fame even greater than it is; the portrait of me is perfect!"

When the courtiers heard this, and saw the friendly hand-shake, their jealousy of the artist was beyond bounds. Their one thought was, how could they safely do something to humiliate him. They dared not pick flaws in the portrait statue, for the prince had declared it perfect. But at last one of them said, with an air of great frankness, "Indeed, Herr Grupello, the portrait of his Royal Highness is perfect; but permit me to say that the statue of the horse is not quite so successful: the head is too large; it is out of proportion."

"No," said another, "the horse is really not so successful; the turn of the neck, there, is awkward."

"If you would change the right hind-foot, Herr Grupello," said a third, "it would be an improvement."

Still another found fault with the horse's tail.

The artist listened, quietly. When they had all finished, he turned to the prince and said, "Your courtiers, prince, find a good many flaws in the statue of the horse; will you permit me to keep it a few days more, to do what I can with it?"

The Elector assented, and the artist ordered a temporary screen to be built around the statue, so that his assistants could work undisturbed. For several days the sound of hammering came steadily from behind the enclosure. The courtiers, who took care to pass that way, often, were delighted. Each one said to himself, "I must have been right, really; the artist himself sees that something was wrong; now I shall have credit for saving the prince's portrait by my artistic taste!"

Once more the artist summoned the prince and his courtiers, and once more the statue was unveiled. Again the Elector exclaimed at its beauty, and then he turned to his courtiers, one after another, to see what they had to say.

"Perfect!" said the first. "Now that the horse's head is in proportion, there is not a flaw."

"The change in the neck was just what was needed," said the second; "it is very graceful now."

"The rear right foot is as it should be, now," said a third, "and it adds so much to the beauty of the whole!"

The fourth said that he considered the tail greatly improved.

"My courtiers are much pleased now," said the prince to Herr Grupello; "they think the statue much improved by the changes you have made."

Herr Grupello smiled a little. "I am glad they are pleased," he said, "but the fact is, I have changed nothing!"

"What do you mean?" said the prince in surprise. "Have we not heard the sound of hammering every day? What were you hammering at then?"

"I was hammering at the reputation of your courtiers, who found fault simply because they were jealous," said the artist. "And I rather think that their reputation is pretty well hammered to pieces!"

It was, indeed. The Elector laughed heartily, but the courtiers slunk away, one after another, without a word.

PRINCE CHERRY[30]

There was once an old king, so wise and kind and true that the most powerful good fairy of his land visited him and asked him to name the dearest wish of his heart, that she might grant it.

"Surely you know it," said the good king; "it is for my only son, Prince Cherry; do for him whatever you would have done for me."

"Gladly," said the great fairy; "choose what I shall give him. I can make him the richest, the most beautiful, or the most powerful prince in the world; choose."

"None of those things are what I want," said the king. "I want only that he shall be good. Of what use will it be to him to be beautiful, rich, or powerful, if he grows into a bad man? Make him the best prince in the world, I beg you!"

"Alas, I cannot make him good," said the fairy; "he must do that for himself. I can give him good advice, reprove him when he does wrong, and punish him if he will not punish himself; I can and will be his best friend, but I cannot make him good unless he wills it."

The king was sad to hear this, but he rejoiced in the friendship of the fairy for his son. And when he died, soon after, he was happy to know that he left Prince Cherry in her hands.

Prince Cherry grieved for his father, and often lay awake at night, thinking of him. One night, when he was all alone in his room, a soft and lovely light suddenly shone before him, and a beautiful vision stood at his side. It was the good fairy. She was clad in robes of dazzling white, and on her shining hair she wore a wreath of white roses.

"I am the Fairy Candide," she said to the prince. "I promised your father that I would be your best friend, and as long as you live I shall watch over your happiness. I have brought you a gift; it is not wonderful to look at, but it has a wonderful power for your welfare; wear it, and let it help you."

As she spoke, she placed a small gold ring on the prince's little finger. "This ring," she said, "will help you to be good; when you do evil, it will prick you, to remind you. If you do not heed its warnings a worse thing will happen to you, for I shall become your enemy." Then she vanished.

Prince Cherry wore his ring, and said nothing to anyone of the fairy's gift. It did not prick him for a long time, because he was good and merry and happy. But Prince Cherry had been rather spoiled by his nurse when he was a child; she had always said to him that when he should become king he could do exactly as he pleased. Now, after a while, he began to find out that this was not true, and it made him angry.

The first time that he noticed that even a king could not always have his own way was on a day when he went hunting. It happened that he got no game. This put him in such a bad temper that he grumbled and scolded all the way home. The little gold ring began to feel tight and uncomfortable. When he reached the palace his pet dog ran to meet him.

"Go away!" said the prince, crossly.

But the little dog was so used to being petted that he only jumped up on his master, and tried to kiss his hand. The prince turned and kicked the little creature. At the instant, he felt a sharp prick in his little finger, like a pin prick.

"What nonsense!" said the prince to himself. "Am I not king of the whole land? May I not kick my own dog, if I choose? What evil is there in that?"

A silver voice spoke in his ear: "The king of the land has a right to do good, but not evil; you have been guilty of bad temper and of cruelty to-day; see that you do better to-morrow."

The prince turned sharply, but no one was to be seen; yet he recognised the voice as that of Fairy Candide.

He followed her advice for a little, but presently he forgot, and the ring pricked him so sharply that his finger had a drop of blood on it. This happened again and again, for the prince grew more self-willed and headstrong every day; he had some bad friends, too, who urged him on, in the hope that he would ruin himself and give them a chance to seize the throne. He treated his people carelessly and his servants cruelly, and everything he wanted he felt that he must have.

The ring annoyed him terribly; it was embarrassing for a king to have a drop of blood on his finger all the time! At last he took the ring off and put it out of sight. Then he thought he should be perfectly happy, having his own way; but instead, he grew more unhappy as he grew less good. Whenever he was crossed, or could not have his own way instantly, he flew into a passion.

Finally, he wanted something that he really could not have. This time it was a most beautiful young girl, named Zelia; the prince saw her, and loved her so much that he wanted at once to make her his queen. To his great astonishment, she refused.

"Am I not pleasing to you?" asked the prince in surprise.

"You are very handsome, very charming, prince," said Zelia; "but you are not like the good king, your father; I fear you would make me very miserable if I were your queen."

In a great rage, Prince Cherry ordered the young girl to be put in prison; and the key of her dungeon he kept. He told one of his friends, a wicked man who flattered him for his own purposes, about the thing, and asked his advice.

"Are you not king?" said the bad friend. "May you not do as you will? Keep the girl in a dungeon till she does as you command, and if she will not, sell her as a slave."

"But would it not be a disgrace for me to harm an innocent creature?" said the prince.

"It would be a disgrace to you to have it said that one of your subjects dared disobey you!" said the courtier.

He had cleverly touched the prince's worst trait, his pride. Prince Cherry went at once to Zelia's dungeon, prepared to do this cruel thing.

Zelia was gone. No one had the key save the prince himself; yet she was gone. The only person who could have dared to help her, thought the prince, was his old tutor, Suliman, the only man left who ever rebuked him for anything. In fury, he ordered Suliman to be put in fetters and brought before him.

As his servants left him, to carry out the wicked order, there was a clash, as of thunder, in the room, and then a blinding light. Fairy Candide stood before him. Her beautiful face was stern, and her silver voice rang like a trumpet, as she said, "Wicked and selfish prince, you have become baser than the beasts you hunt; you are furious as a lion, revengeful as a serpent, greedy as a wolf, and brutal as a bull; take, therefore, the shape of those beasts whom you resemble!"

With horror, the prince felt himself being transformed into a monster. He tried to rush upon the fairy and kill her, but she had vanished with her words. As he stood, her voice came from the air, saying, sadly, "Learn to conquer your pride by being in submission to your own subjects." At the same moment, Prince Cherry felt himself being transported to a distant forest, where he was set down by a clear stream. In the water he saw his own terrible image; he had the head of a lion, with bull's horns, the feet of a wolf, and a tail like a serpent. And as he gazed in horror, the fairy's voice whispered, "Your soul has become more ugly than your shape is; you yourself have deformed it."

The poor beast rushed away from the sound of her words, but in a moment he stumbled into a trap, set by bear-catchers. When the trappers found him they were delighted to have caught a curiosity, and they immediately dragged him to the palace courtyard. There he heard the whole court buzzing with gossip. Prince Cherry had been struck by lightning and killed, was the news, and the five favourite courtiers had struggled to make themselves rulers, but the people had refused them, and offered the crown to Suliman, the good old tutor.

Even as he heard this, the prince saw Suliman on the steps of the palace, speaking to the people. "I will take the crown to keep in trust," he said. "Perhaps the prince is not dead."

"He was a bad king; we do not want him back," said the people.

"I know his heart," said Suliman, "it is not all bad; it is tainted, but not corrupt; perhaps he will repent and come back to us a good king."

When the beast heard this, it touched him so much that he stopped tearing at his chains, and became gentle. He let his keepers lead him away to the royal menagerie without hurting them.

Life was very terrible to the prince, now, but he began to see that he had brought all his sorrow on himself, and he tried to bear it patiently. The worst to bear was the cruelty of the keeper. At last, one night, this keeper was in great danger; a tiger got loose, and attacked him. "Good enough! Let him die!" thought Prince Cherry. But when he saw how helpless the keeper was, he repented, and sprang to help. He killed the tiger and saved the keeper's life.

As he crouched at the keeper's feet, a voice said, "Good actions never go unrewarded!" And the terrible monster was changed into a pretty little white dog.

The keeper carried the beautiful little dog to the court and told the story, and from then on, Cherry was carefully treated, and had the best of everything. But in order to keep the little dog from growing, the queen ordered that he should be fed very little, and that was pretty hard for the poor prince. He was often half starved, although so much petted.

One day he had carried his crust of bread to a retired spot in the palace woods, where he loved to be, when he saw a poor old woman hunting for roots, and seeming almost starved.

"Poor thing," he thought, "she is even more hungry than I"; and he ran up and dropped the crust at her feet.

The woman ate it, and seemed greatly refreshed.

Cherry was glad of that, and he was running happily back to his kennel when he heard cries of distress, and suddenly he saw some rough men dragging along a young girl, who was weeping and crying for help. What was his horror to see that the young girl was Zelia! Oh, how he wished he were the monster once more, so that he could kill the men and rescue her! But he could do nothing except bark, and bite at the heels of the wicked men. That did not stop them; they drove him off, with blows, and carried Zelia into a palace in the wood.

Poor Cherry crouched by the steps, and watched. His heart was full of pity and rage. But suddenly he thought, "I was as bad as these men; I myself put Zelia in prison, and would have treated her worse still, if I had not been prevented." The thought made him so sorry and ashamed that he repented bitterly the evil he had done.

Presently a window opened, and Cherry saw Zelia lean out and throw down a piece of meat. He seized it and was just going to devour it, when the old woman to whom he had given his crust snatched it away and took him in her arms. "No, you shall not eat it, you poor little thing," she said, "for every bit of food in that house is poisoned."

At the same moment, a voice said, "Good actions never go unrewarded!" And instantly Prince Cherry was transformed into a little white dove.

With great joy, he flew to the open palace window to seek out his Zelia, to try to help her. But though he hunted in every room, no Zelia was to be found. He had to fly away, without seeing her. He wanted more than anything else to find her, and stay near her, so he flew out into the world, to seek her.

He sought her in many lands, until one day, in a far eastern country, he found her sitting in a tent, by the side of an old, white-haired hermit. Cherry was wild with delight. He flew to her shoulder, caressed her hair with his beak, and cooed in her ear.

"You dear, lovely little thing!" said Zelia. "Will you stay with me? If you will, I will love you always."

"Ah, Zelia, see what you have done!" laughed the hermit. At that instant, the white dove vanished, and Prince Cherry stood there, as handsome and charming as ever, and with a look of kindness and modesty in his eyes which had never been there before. At the same time, the hermit stood up, his flowing hair changed to shining gold, and his face became a lovely woman's face; it was the Fairy Candide. "Zelia has broken your spell," she said to the prince, "as I meant she should, when you were worthy of her love."

Zelia and Prince Cherry fell at the fairy's feet. But with a beautiful smile she bade them come to their kingdom. In a trice, they were transported to the prince's palace, where King Suliman greeted them with tears of joy. He gave back the throne with all his heart, and King Cherry ruled again, with Zelia for his queen.

He wore the little gold ring all the rest of his life, but never once did it have to prick him hard enough to make his finger bleed.

THE GOLD IN THE ORCHARD[31]

There was once a farmer who had a fine olive orchard. He was very industrious, and the farm always prospered under his care. But he knew that his three sons despised the farm work, and were eager to make wealth fast, through adventure.

When the farmer was old, and felt that his time had come to die, he called the three sons to him and said, "My sons, there is a pot of gold hidden in the olive orchard. Dig for it, if you wish it."

The sons tried to get him to tell them in what part of the orchard the gold was hidden; but he would tell them nothing more.

After the farmer was dead, the sons went to work to find the pot of gold; since they did not know where the hiding-place was, they agreed to begin in a line, at one end of the orchard, and to dig until one of them should find the money.

They dug until they had turned up the soil from one end of the orchard to the other, round the tree-roots and between them. But no pot of gold was to be found. It seemed as if some one must have stolen it, or as if the farmer had been wandering in his wits. The three sons were bitterly disappointed to have all their work for nothing.

The next olive season, the olive trees in the orchard bore more fruit than they had ever given before; the fine cultivating they had had from the digging brought so much fruit, and of so fine a quality, that when it was sold it gave the sons a whole pot of gold!

And when they saw how much money had come from the orchard, they suddenly understood what the wise father had meant when he said, "There is gold hidden in the orchard; dig for it."

MARGARET OF NEW ORLEANS

If you ever go to the beautiful city of New Orleans, somebody will be sure to take you down into the old business part of the city, where there are banks and shops and hotels, and show you a statue which stands in a little square there. It is the statue of a woman, sitting in a low chair, with her arms around a child, who leans against her. The woman is not at all pretty: she wears thick, common shoes, a plain dress, with a little shawl, and a sun-bonnet; she is stout and short, and her face is a square-chinned Irish face; but her eyes look at you like your mother's.

Now there is something very surprising about this statue: it was the first one that was ever made in America in honour of a woman. Even in Europe there are not many monuments to women, and most of the few are to great queens or princesses, very beautiful and very richly dressed. You see, this statue in New Orleans is not quite like anything else.

It is the statue of a woman named Margaret. Her whole name was Margaret Haughery, but no one in New Orleans remembers her by it, any more than you think of your dearest sister by her full name; she is just Margaret. This is her story, and it tells why people made a monument for her.

When Margaret was a tiny baby, her father and mother died, and she was adopted by two young people as poor and as kind as her own parents. She lived with them until she grew up. Then she married, and had a little baby of her own. But very soon her husband died, and then the baby died, too, and Margaret was all alone in the world. She was poor, but she was strong, and knew how to work.

All day, from morning until evening, she ironed clothes in a laundry. And every day, as she worked by the window, she saw the little motherless children from the orphan asylum, near by, working and playing about. After a while, there came a great sickness upon the city, and so many mothers and fathers died that there were more orphans than the asylum could possibly take care of. They needed a good friend, now. You would hardly think, would you, that a poor woman who worked in a laundry could be much of a friend to them? But Margaret was. She went straight to the kind Sisters who had the asylum and told them she was going to give them part of her wages and was going to work for them, besides. Pretty soon she had worked so hard that she had some money saved from her wages. With this, she bought two cows and a little delivery cart. Then she carried her milk to her customers in the little cart every morning; and as she went, she begged the pieces of food left over from the hotels and rich houses, and brought it back in the cart to the hungry children in the asylum. In the very hardest times that was often all the food the poor children had.

A part of the money Margaret earned went every week to the asylum, and after a few years that was made very much larger and better. Margaret was so careful and so good at business that, in spite of her giving, she bought more cows and earned more money. With this, she built a home for orphan babies; she called it her baby house.

After a time, Margaret had a chance to get a bakery, and then she became a bread-woman instead of a milk-woman. She carried the bread just as she had carried the milk, in her cart. And still she kept giving money to the asylum. Then the great war came, the Civil War. In all the trouble and sickness and fear of that time, Margaret drove her cart of bread; and somehow she had always enough to give the starving soldiers, and for her babies, beside what she sold. And despite all this, she earned enough so that when the war was over she built a big steam factory for her bread. By this time everybody in the city knew her. The children all over the city loved her; the business men were proud of her; the poor people all came to her for advice. She used to sit at the open door of her office, in a calico gown and a little shawl, and give a good word to everybody, rich or poor.

Then, by and by, one day, Margaret died. And when it was time to read her will, the people found that, with all her giving, she had still saved a great deal of money, and that she had left every penny of it to the different orphan asylums of the city,—each one of them was given something. Whether they were for white children or black, for Jews, Catholics, or Protestants, made no difference; for Margaret always said, "They are all orphans alike." And just think, dears, that splendid, wise will was signed with a cross instead of a name, for Margaret had never learned to read or write!

When the people of New Orleans knew that Margaret was dead, they said, "She was a mother to the motherless; she was a friend to those who had no friends; she had wisdom greater than schools can teach; we will not let her memory go from us." So they made a statue of her, just as she used to look, sitting in her own office door, or driving in her own little cart. And there it stands to-day, in memory of the great love and the great power of plain Margaret Haughery, of New Orleans.

THE DAGDA'S HARP

You know, dears, in the old countries there are many fine stories about things which happened so very long ago that nobody knows exactly how much of them is true. Ireland is like that. It is so old that even as long ago as four thousand years it had people who dug in the mines, and knew how to weave cloth and to make beautiful ornaments out of gold, and who could fight and make laws; but we do not know just where they came from, nor exactly how they lived. These people left us some splendid stories about their kings, their fights, and their beautiful women; but it all happened such a long time ago that the stories are mixtures of things that really happened and what people said about them, and we don't know just which is which. The stories are called *legends*. One of the prettiest legends is the story I am going to tell you about the Dagda's harp.

It is said that there were two quite different kinds of people in Ireland: one set of people with long dark hair and dark eyes, called Fomorians— they carried long slender spears made of golden bronze when they fought— and another race of people who were golden-haired and blue-eyed, and who carried short, blunt, heavy spears of dull metal.

The golden-haired people had a great chieftain who was also a kind of high priest, who was called the Dagda. And this Dagda had a wonderful magic harp. The harp was beautiful to look upon, mighty in size, made of rare wood, and ornamented with gold and jewels; and it had wonderful music in its strings, which only the Dagda could call out. When the men were going out to battle, the Dagda would set up his magic harp and sweep his hand across the strings, and a war song would ring out which would make every warrior buckle on his armour, brace his knees, and shout, "Forth to the fight!" Then, when the men came back from the battle, weary and wounded, the Dagda would take his harp and strike a few chords, and as the magic music stole out upon the air, every man forgot his weariness and the smart of his wounds, and thought of the honour he had won, and of the comrade who had died beside him, and of the safety of his wife and children. Then the song would swell out louder, and every warrior would remember only the glory he had helped win for the king; and each man would rise at the great table, his cup in his hand, and shout "Long live the King!"

There came a time when the Fomorians and the golden-haired men were at war; and in the midst of a great battle, while the Dagda's hall was not so well guarded as usual, some of the chieftains of the Fomorians stole the great harp from the wall, where it hung, and fled away with it. Their wives and children and some few of their soldiers went with them, and they fled fast and far through the night, until they were a long way from the battlefield. Then they thought they were safe, and they turned aside into a vacant castle, by the road, and sat down to a banquet, hanging the stolen harp on the wall.

The Dagda, with two or three of his warriors, had followed hard on their track. And while they were in the midst of their banqueting, the door was suddenly burst open, and the Dagda stood there, with his men. Some of the Fomorians sprang to their feet, but before any of them could grasp a weapon, the Dagda called out to his harp on the wall, "Come to me, O my harp!"

The great harp recognised its master's voice, and leaped from the wall. Whirling through the hall, sweeping aside and killing the men who got in its way, it sprang to its master's hand. And the Dagda took his harp and swept his hand across the strings in three great, solemn chords. The harp answered with the magic Music of Tears. As the wailing harmony smote upon the air, the women of the Fomorians bowed their heads and wept bitterly, the strong men turned their faces aside, and the little children sobbed.

Again the Dagda touched the strings, and this time the magic Music of Mirth leaped from the harp. And when they heard that Music of Mirth, the young warriors of the Fomorians began to laugh; they laughed till the cups fell from their grasp, and the spears dropped from their hands, while the wine flowed from the broken bowls; they laughed until their limbs were helpless with excess of glee.

Once more the Dagda touched his harp, but very, very softly. And now a music stole forth as soft as dreams, and as sweet as joy: it was the magic Music of Sleep. When they heard that, gently, gently, the Fomorian women bowed their heads in slumber; the little children crept to their mothers' laps; the old men nodded; and the young warriors drooped in their seats and closed their eyes: one after another all the Fomorians sank into sleep.

When they were all deep in slumber, the Dagda took his magic harp, and he and his golden-haired warriors stole softly away, and came in safety to their own homes again.

www.ingramcontent.com/pod-product-compliance
Lightning Source LLC
Chambersburg PA
CBHW080909190726
48294CB00008B/2019